Dreaming OUTSIDE THE LINES

Dreaming Outside the Lines

M. ROSE ELLIOTT

Copyright © 2026 by M. Rose Elliott

All rights reserved. No part of this book may be used or reproduced in any form without written permission except in the case of brief quotations in critical articles or reviews.

This book is a work of fiction. Any names, characters, places, and incidents are products of the author's imagination, or are used fictitiously, and are not to be construed as real. Any resemblance to actual events, locals, or persons, living or dead, is entirely coincidental.

MEDICAL DISCLAIMER: Any medical information, diagnoses, treatments, procedures, or outcomes described are presented for fictional purposes only and are not intended as medical advice. The author is not a medical professional. Readers should seek advice from qualified professionals for any health-related concerns.

No generative Artificial Intelligence (AI) was used in the writing of this book.

Editing by Donna Marie West

Interior Formatting and Artwork by Aubrey Labitigan | Facebook.com/designjai

Cover design by Sabrina Watts of Enchanted Ink Studio | www.enchantedinkstudio.com.

Paperback: 979-8-9941037-1-5

Ebook: 979-8-9941037-2-2

*To my dreams - thank you for adding
color to my life.*

Prologue

VALANCY

Here is a place I can love without effort. I gaze about the dense, tree-filled park, golden beams of sunlight filtering through the leaves, illuminating dust motes in the air. The trees are older than those in the neighborhood I just came through; they cast the park into denser shade, which is a relief in the summer heat. As I head to the opposite corner where I can see a fun-looking playground, I admire the space around me. There are open lawns for games, a quaint pavilion people probably use for events, and colorful flower beds and wooden benches placed thoughtfully. The whole effect is cozy, arboreal peace, a far cry from the cookie cutter manicured neighborhoods surrounding the park.

For the first time since moving here, I feel curiosity and interest. The tension in my chest loosens, and I'm relieved that I'll be able to go home and tell Mom that I found something to be excited about. She'll probably be glad to hear it; she has been worried about me, I think.

Twenty minutes ago, when the kitchen door shut kindly but firmly behind me, I wasn't sure what she was hoping I would find outside. The aspect from the door looking out at our pristine, postage stamp-sized lawn wasn't promising. For a minute, I considered giving up and going back inside, but I want to do my part to adapt. Seeing the lace curtain in the window twitch prompted me down the path to the sidewalk, hefting my small shoulder bag more securely across my flat chest. I knew she was checking to see if I was still standing on the stoop. She has faith in me that I don't feel right now.

Until I followed the bend in the road and saw the park, I wasn't feeling very hopeful. Some adult neighbors were out, but they only gave me a cursory nod or a mild greeting. I didn't see any other kids.

Dad says that moving here is a new opportunity. He's excited about his new job and comes home every night with exciting stories about work. Mom has already found a group she meets with once a week to work together on craft projects. She seems optimistic. I wish I felt the same. Even Tanner has some sports camp he's going to.

The day after fourth grade ended, we packed up everything and moved. There's still two months left of summer, but there's no summer art camp here like there was in Fayette, and I don't know any other kids. My friends Molly and Jesamine are far away. I'm not sure if I'll ever see them again. Maybe a new family moved into our old house, and their kids get to play with them now. These were my thoughts as I continued walking through the neighborhood. I was fighting the tears stinging the corners of my eyes by the time I saw the park.

I'm almost at the playground, and I feel a spring in my step that I haven't felt in weeks, my impending tears forgotten. The playground is one of those fancy metal-and-wooden ones with hidden areas and secret tubes so you can talk to someone echoey on the other side. By the time I get to the jungle gym, I'm jogging in anticipation. I fling my bag on a bench and sprint over to the monkey bars. I shimmy up and hand-over-hand my way across. A giggle of joy escapes my mouth. This feels good.

I drop into the sand on the other side, falling to my hands and knees. When I stand up and look around after wiping my hands on my shirt, I'm surprised to find a boy standing in front of me. Older, probably in sixth or seventh grade, he's wearing a nerdy video game shirt and blue jeans with the knees torn out. His hair is too long. I bet his parents are waiting until the end of summer to get it cut again, so it stands up in a lopsided fan where he brushes it out of his eyes.

We stare at each other for a moment. I'm shy around new people; I hope he'll say something before I have to. He suddenly smiles a full grin, which makes me feel even more awkward because I'm currently missing my canines and compared to him, I feel like a little kid. I smile back with my lips held firmly together. He doesn't seem fazed by my weird behavior.

"Do you want to look at the tadpoles in the pond?" he asks eagerly.

In the ten years of my life, I can't say that I've ever prioritized inspecting tadpoles, but in this moment, it sounds like heaven. Being asked to do anything with someone close to my age is a relief from the isolation I've felt these past weeks.

"There's a pond?" I question, looking around. I hadn't seen one on my way through the park.

"Yep! Over there." He points to a corner I didn't walk near. I can see foliage and rocks surrounding an open area. Before I can say anything else, he jogs off in that direction. I don't think twice before running after him, my saddle shoes pounding on the grassy dirt. He has a head start and his legs are longer. I don't catch up to him until he stops and bends over at the edge of what I can now see clearly is indeed a little pond. I crouch down beside him, my shoes sinking into the muck, and peer into the murky water. All I see is wafting slime. I wrinkle my nose; there's a funny smell too.

"Look!" He holds his finger down near the surface, and as I lean precariously forward on my toes to see better, my shoes squelch. I gasp when I spot the bulbous little bodies with their ethereal tails swimming around in the warm shallows. The smell and slime are forgotten. I reach my finger out to try and touch one, but it darts away before my finger breaks the surface of the water. It returns as soon as I take my hand away.

We squat in companionable silence, watching the baby amphibians. Finally, mustering my courage, I say, "I'm Valancy."

He looks over and smiles. "I'm Jeremy. Are you new?"

"Yeah. We just moved here this month."

"Hey, don't be sad, you're going to love living here. I've lived here my whole life, and it's the best." He looks at me kindly, and for the first time since moving here, I believe that things might be okay again after all.

The shadows are getting long by the time I head back to the playground to grab my bag. Jeremy saw me throw it and reminded me to go get it before heading home. As I pull it over my shoulder, I turn to wave again. He's in the neighborhood on the opposite side of the park from where I entered. He has been walking backward, making sure I went back for my bag. He flings his arm in the air and fans it back and forth when he sees me wave, then turns and jogs off down the street. With a smile on my face and a lightness in my heart, I head back to my house.

The worry lines in Mom's forehead smooth when I push through the kitchen door and dump my bag on a chair. I can hear the TV in the den, as I plop into a slat-backed chair at the table. Mom places a glass of orange juice in front of me before going back to preparing dinner. She glances over while dicing celery.

"Did you have fun?" she asks.

"I found a park and met a boy named Jeremy. We watched tadpoles and played tag and climbed a tree." I wiggle excitedly in my seat, remembering the baby frogs.

If my mom feels any concern, she doesn't let it show. "That's wonderful, Valley, I'm glad you made a friend." She smiles over her shoulder at me. Only my family calls me Valley.

I grin back before taking a huge gulp of my juice.

At dinner, my parents discuss work and projects, but they make a point of including Tanner and me in the conversation. Tanner talks about his team and I happily tell them about my new friend and the beautiful park. I catch them sharing a look of relief when they think I'm not watching.

Dad says, "Maybe being more active and having a friend will help those dreams you've been having." Mom's forehead creases and she cuts resolutely into her meatloaf.

"Maybe," I acknowledge, "although I think they're kinda cool. It'd be neat to tell kids that I have dreams that feel real."

Dad clearly doesn't know how to respond to such a statement. He just nods and turns back to his meal.

***

And so began a happy summer and a wonderful, lifelong friendship. Jeremy and I became best friends that summer, which continued when the school year started. We were always in the same district and usually in the same school except when he moved on a year ahead of me. He was my first dance in junior high, and my date to senior prom because all the other guys were lame. Going to prom with your best friend is the best. We won all the fake money in the casino.

We went to the same community college. I took two years and he took three because he was working part time. We entered the University of New Mexico the same year and graduated together in May 2011, him with a degree in computer science and me with a double major in studio art and business. His mom and my dad sat together during the ceremony and overwhelmed us with balloon bouquets and purple orchid leis afterward. We got jobs in the same town where our families still lived, and we still caught up with each other regularly for lunch and game nights and family gatherings. Our friendship ebbed and flowed, but we never completely lost touch.

Eventually, we were both sick of living with our families, but the economy was awful. Five years ago, we decided to become roommates and rented a small house together. Our house is a tiny two-bedroom in an older part of town. I love the huge trees with the small houses nestled back from the road. We're close to a nature reserve, which is great for easy access to hiking. Jeremy commutes to Albuquerque now, but he's close enough to work that he doesn't feel any need to move.

Now, let me stop you right there. Jeremy and I have never been romantically involved. Okay, so maybe there was that one time in college, but aside from that mistake, we've always been just friends. The best of friends. I don't know what I would do without him in my life.

Many Years Later

ADRIAN

"Goodnight…" Their voice catches on the light evening breeze and carries my name away.

I wave to a retreating back as I turn for home. Everything is reverting, but I still feel on edge. Today involved too much spinning. My head is still reeling and I feel slightly nauseous. Sometimes I think I'm not cut out for this job. Maybe I should ask for a transfer somewhere without a carnival. For a moment, I think fondly of the corporate office building I used to work in, but then I shrug. Honestly, it doesn't matter. The work is always the same, and I'm as likely to feel woozy from a fast elevator as I am from a ride.

The streets are empty as I make my way through the city. Lights shine out of some windows high above me, and occasionally I hear distant sounds of activity, but nothing stirs along my path.

Climbing the stairs to my apartment feels more fatiguing

than usual. Today took it out of me. I think back over the visitors I met with, but none of them stand out. Their requirements were typical, their stories normal, unique only in that they all wanted to go on the rides. My head may currently disagree, but the rest of me has no complaints. It was simple.

I push open my door. The soothing blues and browns greet me, and I breathe a sigh of contentment. It's good to be home. I shrug out of my jacket and hang it by the door. As dinner warms up, I flop on the sofa. I make the mistake of closing my eyes. They won't be reopening anytime soon.

I'm behind the wheel, driving down a long, dark stretch of highway. The radio is blaring, and I pinch the bridge of my nose and scrunch my eyes for a second to relieve the strain. There's a car up ahead, but I'm not catching up. The flat desert scenery flows by, lulling my senses until I worry I might be a hazard, but there's nowhere to stop.

The sun is up by the time I finally start to see promising signs of civilization. Taking the first exit, I pull into the parking lot of a coffee shop bakery. Sammy's, the red plastic sign proclaims. The lot is mostly empty. I ease my car in next to a small red hatchback.

My body screams in relief when I stand up, and I can't resist stretching my hands up above my head. The sun and fresh air feel good on my skin that's been bathed in the unnatural breeze of the car's air conditioner.

I go inside, taking my place behind a woman with a ponytail who's currently placing her order. She's getting three bear claws. The attendant helps her and then asks me what I want. The rows of pastries shine with glaze, and I spend a moment admiring them. There's no one behind me; I can take my time. The employee takes a sip of her coffee while she waits for my decision. Finally, I know what I want. As I open my mouth to place my order, my pager dings.

Startled, I raise my head from the sofa and look at the bright kitchen window. It's morning. My stomach rumbles. I curse myself for falling asleep on the sofa and for not eating dinner. My pager chimes again, and I look at it in exasperation. Blast! I'm primary for this visitor, which means I'm needed immediately. I give my kitchen a despondent glance before grabbing my jacket and dashing out the door.

Chapter 1

The bright morning light that's unique to an overcast day does to my eyes what the alarm is doing to my ears. Groaning, I roll over in defiance of the day, trying to hang onto the last remnants of my dream. It was the first normal dream I've had in a while, and I want to savor it. My alarm has other ideas. I fumble for my phone and sit up, bleary-eyed. I'm not much of a morning person.

I'm at the counter boiling water for tea when Jeremy prances in. Okay, so he doesn't actually prance, but his perky morning person energy feels like prancing to my still waking brain. He's always irritatingly awake and well rested in the morning. Fortunately, he's well aware that it takes me a solid forty-five minutes to warm up to the day. While pulling milk from the fridge for cereal, he says good morning.

"You want a cup?" I ask, gesturing to the water that's started to undulate.

"No time. Thanks, though. I have to get to work."

I nod and turn back to my tea preparations.

Jeremy scarfs down his breakfast and hollers a quick "Bye!" as I'm setting my tea and toast on the table. Before I have a chance to respond, the door clicks shut.

I'm just as glad to not have to interact. Peaceful mornings before work where I'm alone in the house are my favorite. Breakfasts with Jeremy can be pleasant too, but today I'm glad for the reprieve. Contemplating the view out the window while sipping my tea, I'm pleased to see it has started to rain.

***

Wipers on medium speed, I pull into The Paint Palette's lot, feeling glad that my commute was uneventful and that mine is the first car here. Being the first one in means I can take a few minutes to turn on the lights and settle myself before everyone else shows up.

I'm glad I decided to wear a light sweater and jeans today. The rain is making the air chilly. As I unlock the door, I glance over at Elton's bench and notice it's getting drenched. Making a mental note to move it under the overhang once the weather is more agreeable, I drop my items on the front desk and start turning on lights and checking the galleries.

The Paint Palette Gallery, and those related to it in other

towns around the West, were founded by the grandfather of my supervisor Mark's boss, Leondra Smith-Cummings, in 1968 as a place for artists to have a space to show their work. Grandfather Cummings wasn't an artist himself, but he loved the art culture, particularly during the 1960s hippy era. He had a significant personal inheritance and was doing well for himself as a lawyer. Funding a gallery was within his means. He started with one in California and within fifteen years, he was able to expand to a moderately sized chain of twenty galleries. Because the organization remains small and spread out, each gallery has its own name and style that reflects the local color and personalities of its community. The hippy vibe is only still strong with some of the oldest locations. The rest, including The Paint Palette, are much more contemporary. Because we're located in New Mexico, our art often has a colorful Western vibe.

The Palette, as we fondly call it among ourselves, has four main areas. When a customer walks in, they're greeted by whomever is running the front desk, which is in the Main Gallery. The Main Gallery is the largest room and has an assortment of works on display. There is a large jewelry counter in the center, which is divided into smaller subsections for individual artists. Around the jewelry island, there are some textile arts such as scarves and fabric flowers on stands and small displays.

The walls of the Main Gallery are filled with all manner of visual arts, loosely separated by artist. Sometimes the walls get crowded. To help keep the delineation clear, we try to arrange them in such a way that different styles are adjacent to each other. The effect can be an assault to the senses, but I love the colors and the vast assortment of items to look at. Customers often comment on how much they enjoy the visual rush.

In comparison, the individual galleries—Cottontail, Bighorn, and Roadrunner—are calmer spaces. They're offshoots of the Main Gallery and have additional connecting archways between each other. These galleries are available for artists to use for individual or small group shows. We have them on a rotating schedule; each gallery is set for a three-month period, but only one gallery is changed out per month. This prevents The Palette as a whole from ever giving the appearance of complete disarray.

All the artists in The Palette are juried in, and we take a modest commission on any pieces they sell. To use the individual galleries, they fill out applications for solo exhibits. For the smaller areas within our Main Gallery, they just bring in items or email pictures and we decide what we want to include in our display, with Mark having the final say.

Typically, our vibe is colorful Western contemporary, but sometimes we have an outlier show. I'm always pleased when these shows do well too. I take personal pride knowing that I've helped change the image of our gallery for the better by suggesting we give more unusual exhibits a chance. Mark was hesitant at first, but he's always willing to give new ideas a try once. Now that he has seen how successful something different can be, he's more open to additional suggestions.

I take my time as I make my way around The Palette, turning on lights, checking displays, admiring pieces I haven't seen before. It's a soothing way to start the day. Being the first one here is a big motivator for me to get up with my alarm in the morning. Once I'm done, I grab my items from the front desk and take them to our office area in the back of the building.

Daphne is the next to arrive. She unceremoniously drops her lunch bag in the fridge, tosses her cardigan over the back of her chair, and goes to the kitchenette to brew coffee. Once she has got the process going, she comes back into our shared desk area and flops down in her chair.

"Good morning?" I ask, glancing over at her with a smile.

She smiles back with a slightly tired look. "Good morning. Just a sec." She hops back up and sounds of coffee preparation emerge from the kitchenette. A couple minutes later, she returns with her steaming mug and inhales the steam. "Mmm…" She takes a sip. "Nothing like rainy weather to make me want all things cozy."

Nodding in agreement, I consider if I already want a second cup of tea.

I've worked with Daphne the longest; she was already here when I was hired. She's a four years younger than me, and we get along well. She has a husband, a son, a dog, and a large extended family. We never hang out outside of work, but we're friends all the same.

"How was your weekend?" I ask. I suspect she had a less than relaxing weekend since her husband, Esteban, had a glorious plan for an "only the four of us" weekend for their little family, including the dog in that number. I'm guessing the trip may have become quite the production, since her son is still pretty young.

She laughs wanly. "It was pretty good. Kinda crazy. I've told you about Esteban and his ideas. But Fred had fun, and it was nice to be at the lake. At least the rain held off until today. How was your weekend? Did you do anything fun?"

I temper my response, knowing it can be hard for her to hear about my much less chaotic life. "It was good. I worked on an artwork and did a lot of cleaning. Jeremy was out with friends most of the time, so I had the house to myself."

She nods with interest and might have inquired further about my current art project, but at that moment Mark bursts in.

Mark is a vibrant and full of life person. He flings open doors more than you would think necessary and is louder than is sometimes comfortable, but he has a heart of pure gold. He's ten years older than me, and we see eye to eye on most things, but occasionally we feel some generational inertia away from each other. Fortunately, that hasn't kept us from doing well together as coworkers.

Today, he's laden with an enormous bunch of sunflowers and a beribboned cellophane box with a massive cream puff inside. Everything is covered in water droplets. "I was at The Farm last night and they had these in their dessert case!" he exclaims without preamble. "I want to eat it, but I absolutely refuse to consume this entire thing by myself." Thrusting the damp cellophane bouquet into Daphne's waiting arms and the creampuff box into mine, he heads to the cabinet and pulls out plates and utensils to start divvying everything up.

Daphne shoots me an amused look as she takes the sunflowers, puts them in a vase, and carries them up front to the table by the door. Their vibrant yellow is cheery, and I approve of Mark's choice for the week. We take turns bringing in fresh flowers for The Palette, and I'm a sucker for yellows and oranges, particularly in contrast to this dreary weather.

Mark finishes the cream puff slicing, or more like smoosh dividing, and pours hot water from the kettle for himself. I cave and make myself another tea too. A creampuff without tea to accompany it would feel blasphemous.

The water kettle is mine, but Mark willingly jumped on the tea bandwagon and even Daphne has a tea now and then once she has satisfied her daily coffee requirement. Mark is also a coffee drinker and has a cup before he gets to work. To not add more caffeine to the mix, he has herbal tea at the office. As he says, he's over forty now and has to watch his caffeine intake, or he won't sleep at night. Mark's personality always seems perpetually hyped up. It's hard to imagine him ever relaxing, with or without the influence of caffeine.

Mornings at work are relaxed because we aren't open to the

public for the first hour. We use it to do urgent matters that are easier without customers, or to relax and catch up with each other. Since this is a chill week with no major initiatives, we have time for a morning get-together. Even on our busier weeks, we can typically have at least one relaxed morning, and on slower weeks we may have two or three. It's one of my favorite parts of the work week.

We traipse out to the back patio laden with our morning goodies. The porch is cheerful with its colorful, mismatched bistro set that was partially donated by my brother Tanner and added to with items from Daphne's aunt. The large roof protects us from the rain. Once we've all settled into our chairs, there is a collective sigh of satisfaction. I'm glad we all like rainy weather. I had a friend in college who was originally from the East Coast. She despised rainy days. It dampened my enthusiasm for inclement weather.

"How were you guys' weekends?" Mark asks, as he relaxes in his seat and takes a sip of tea. He's considerably more relaxed sounding than he was when he blew in a few minutes ago. I open my mouth to respond, but he stops me mid-breath. "Wait! First, let's all try this creampuff!"

This is a valid course of action, and there is a united groan of pleasure as we all dig into our cream puff wedges.

"You are never allowed to buy these again," Daphne says accusingly between mouthfuls.

Mark laughs delightedly, and I chime in that I veto her idea. He has to bring it again.

Silently munching for a while, enjoying our treats and the rain, I'm glad for my hot tea that helps cut the chill in the air. After a few minutes, Mark loops back to his original question. Daphne and I give him brief accounts of our weekend activities and then ask him how his was.

"I went to the Renaissance Fair!" he blurts out, referring to the one that's temporarily set up in the next town over.

"Oh, fun!" Daphne exclaims. "Did you dress up?"

"Yeah, me and my friends Al and Rakesh went, and we all dressed up as knights. They're more into it than me. They made their costumes. It was particularly neat because during the jousting, one of the troubadours was looking for audience participation and picked Rakesh. It's supposed to be an amusing bout where the audience member does some simple sword fighting with one of the cast members, but Rakesh has done some sword fighting classes, which meant they were able to amp up the performance." Mark laughs, savoring the memory.

"Rakesh's the one who bought one of those big abstract blue paintings we had up, right?" I ask.

"Yep! He has that over the mantle in his living room. It's a great fit for his décor. I never tell him how glad we are he took it off our hands." He laughs again. "Those things would not sell!" The three of us laugh, recalling some pieces we'd acquired by mistake that were much larger than anticipated. It was a happy day when we sold the last one at a greatly reduced price.

There's more back and forth conversation and then Daphne rises and starts collecting our dishes. Looking at my watch, I see that it's getting close to opening time. "I'll take the first half of the day up front, if that works for everyone?" I ask.

Daphne and Mark agree.

I unlock the front door and turn on the open sign. A few minutes later, Elton Burrows strolls in, greeting me while closing his umbrella.

"Mornin', Ms. Val. How're you this fine morning?" He props his umbrella next to the door.

I straighten from where I'm organizing some handmade greeting cards and smile at him. Elton is a regular fixture in our town, and since he retired, he often sits on the old painted bench we have out front. Part of our success can be attributed to people seeing Elton and stopping by to say hello.

"Hey there, Mr. Burrows, it's nice to see you this morning. My weekend was good. How was yours?"

"Oh, you know, there was that disappointin' football game, and then my back was achin' a bit, but all in all, I can't complain too much. My wife got me this new shirt, and I'm feelin' snazzy." He accompanies the last word with a little shimmy dance move. What a cutie.

Hawaiian shirts are his signature style, and this new one is especially pretty. It's all coral and white tones with hibiscus and surfboards. He has paired it with some olive-green cargo pants and brown loafers that have gotten a bit damp.

"You're looking fancy today! I like the colors."

"Me too, but I have to be careful tellin' the missus too many compliments about her selection or she'll bury me in four more that all look exactly the same." We share a laugh, and he plops down on a chair placed near the front door with his newspaper and settles in to hang out. He probably won't stay as long today because it's raining and he can't sit outside, but it'll be nice to have some company for a bit while I'm up front.

I go back to the kitchenette and make him a cup of coffee.

"Well, aren't you a doll. Thank you, Ms. Val."

"You're welcome, it's always nice to see you."

"And you, darlin'." He takes a sip and furls his paper again. I return to sorting cards.

***

It's almost time for my lunch, and Daphne will be coming to relieve me soon. As I start to gather my things, the phone rings.

"Hello, thank you for calling The Paint Palette Gallery. This is Valancy, how can I help you?" My phone voice is particularly perky from previously working in a call center.

"Valancy! Just the person I wanted to talk to!" The voice is familiar. "This is Bryce Hampton."

"Oh hey, Mr. Hampton!"

"Bryce, please. 'Mr. Hampton' makes me feel old," he teases.

I laugh easily. "I'll try to remember that." I'm making no promises. "What can I help you with?"

"I was hoping you could tell me when I should come in to set up my show."

"Oh, sure! Let me see." I pull our front desk calendar toward me. "Ms. Galaxy is going to be taking down her show on Thursday, and then we need some time to prep the gallery. Does next Friday work?"

"That's perfect, thanks. I'll probably be in sometime between ten and eleven."

"That will work great." We exchange closing pleasantries and hang up.

I mark the calendar with his arrival window. Since the three of us rotate sitting at the front desk, we try to keep the main calendar updated with anything that the others also need to know.

Daphne appears carrying her green notebook and a novel. "Who was that?"

"Mr. Hampton. He wanted to know when he should bring his art in."

She nods. "I'm excited for his show, but I'm going to miss Ms. Galaxy's. It's been such an enjoyable display. Who do we have in Cottontail after Hampton?"

I check the calendar. "The Torres sisters."

"They don't sound familiar. Have they shown here before?"

"I don't think so. I remember Mark specifically commenting on their interesting style. They incorporate fiber elements into their paintings. It creates a dynamic, rough surface. I think Camila is primarily the painter, and Ximena does the fiber parts."

"Super cool! I love it when we get someone new."

"Me too!" We share a smile. We love The Palette, and it's always gratifying to see how our work and efforts, and those of Mark, have expanded and improved this space. The community has overwhelmed us with their support and love. We've built a reputation for interesting, quality art at a wide range of price points. We offer all kinds of styles and esthetics. People know that when they visit, they'll be able to find something that strikes their fancy.

***

The rain finally stopped in the late afternoon. I'm so fickle when it comes to the weather. I want it to rain, but then once it does, I start to crave the sun again. I suppose it's because whatever the weather is, it means I'm missing out on some other kind.

I don't feel like cooking. I text Jeremy from the parking lot before leaving to see if he wants me to pick up dinner for him too. I'm betting he'll say yes. It's a Monday. My phone vibrates. Called it!

I go through the drive thru for Buster's Burgers and pick up dinner for us. Normally I'm a fries person, but Buster's makes the best onion rings. I'm looking forward to having a quiet evening at home with Jeremy. We're pretty busy, but we see each other regularly in the evenings and on weekends.

"Does your burger have mustard on it?"

"No." I always request mine without. "Why? Does yours?" I ask.

"No." Jeremy pouts. "They must have misunderstood and removed it from both." He goes to the refrigerator and pulls out the mustard bottle. With long-suffering dramatics, he squirts some on his bun and sighs heavily. I giggle. He glares at me. "I see you don't sympathize with my suffering."

"I don't think our mustard is any different than Buster's. I think you'll survive."

"Actually, there is one very significant difference," he pontificates. "Ours is cold."

"Do you want me to microwave it for you to warm it up?"

His aghast expression makes me chuckle again. "Absolutely not!" He holds his burger away from me, protectively. "It's fine the way it is." He takes a bite, looking warily at me, as though I might snatch it from him and warm it without his permission.

I laugh and roll my eyes at him.

When I'm starting to feel pleasantly full, I ask, "How was your day?"

"Not bad. How was yours?" It has been a bit like pulling teeth to get Jeremy to open up lately. We'll have beautifully light moments, like with the mustard, but once I take the conversation in a more personal direction, he clams up. It used to be that if I asked him about work or life, he would naturally expound with all kinds of details. I suspect I know what's causing it, and it's a conversation I'm not yet ready to have.

"We were quiet, just a few patrons today. The rain kept people away, I think. Mostly we just made sure we're all set for our next show."

He nods but doesn't inquire further, focusing on his remaining onion rings.

A couple hours later, I'm in my room staring at the canvas I started working on over the weekend. It has the rudimentary beginning of a painting on it. I have this nagging idea in the back of my mind that I'm feeling compelled to bring to life. It's challenging because the visions I'm imagining are vague and hard to hold onto, which has translated into dark swooshes and splotches so far.

Jeremy knocks lightly. When he hears my acknowledgment, he cracks the door and sticks his head in.

"Shelly at work recommended a show to me. It's got a few full seasons on streaming, and the plot sounds like one you might like too. Do you want to watch the first episode?"

I glance over at him and catch a hopefulness in his expression he quickly masks.

"That sounds good. This artwork is bugging me. A new show would be a nice distraction. Let me clean this up, and I'll be out in a few minutes."

"Sure thing!" He vanishes. Sigh. I miss when he used to ask me about my art and talk to me about my frustrations. I clean up my palette, wash my brushes, and rinse out my paint rags. I hang my apron on a hook by the door.

We watch the first two episodes. Jeremy's coworker was right; this is a good show. By the time we turn off the TV, we're in agreement that we're hooked. Unfortunately, as solidly mid-thirties adults, there is no way we're watching any more tonight.

There are shoes everywhere, mountains of them. Why are there no coral ones? This tent is enormous, but there is nothing in the color I need. Oh well, I guess I'll have to go to the wedding in my hiking boots. I march out of the tent, gauze from my skirt catching on the rough leather of my boots.

Mark and Daphne's wedding is beautiful. Everything is purple, except for Mark's suit, which is white. Daphne's lavender wedding dress is stunning, with coral-colored flowers adorning the flounces. My hiking boots were a bad idea; they clash with my plaid dress. If the wedding has a flood, everyone else will wish they had boots on.

The wedding cream puff is enormous, but the topper keeps sliding down the chocolate sides. It looks like the bride and groom are skiing down a mudslide. Unfortunately, the crowd around it is dense, preventing me from getting a piece. I finally push my way to the front, and a knight brandishes a sword in my face.

My alarm rings.

Rolling over, I squint one eye at the window. Darn it, it's daylight outside. My alarm isn't wrong. I grumble and begrudgingly get out of bed. My brown tabby Bob follows me to the bathroom, weaving his way between my legs as I walk.

Chapter 2
VALANCY

Mark is in before me, and all the lights have been turned on. He's at his desk reading emails and eating a protein bar when I arrive. He's giving off no-nonsense vibes this morning; maybe the scale didn't reflect kindly after yesterday's cream puff. Becoming middle-aged has been a stressor for him, and he worries about his corresponding thickening waistline. I don't think he needs to worry; he's an attractive guy. He has great taste in clothes that always suit him beautifully. He wears his locs to just above his ears and styles them with a rakish part off to one side. But of course, we're always our own worst critic.

"Hey, Mark."

"Hey, good morning," he says absently. "Oh. Daphne is going to be late; she had to take Fred in for some shots."

"That sounds fun." It does not. Daphne's a great mom and Fred is the cutest kid, but I'm not jealous of her motherhood.

His eyes back on his computer screen, Mark's eyebrows crease his forehead vertically in the center. It's unlike him to be terse with words, but I let him be and log in to my computer before going to boil water. I was dragging this morning and ran out of time for breakfast.

"Do you want tea?" I ask, peeking around the corner.

"No, I'm good, thanks."

I bring my mug back to my desk. Yum, I steeped it perfectly. I catch up on my emails and review some pressing items. Mark is still absorbed by his computer and every so often types furiously. After forty-five minutes, I finally break the silence. "What are you working on?"

He looks slightly startled, like he has been caught doing something naughty. "Nothing, really. I had a weird email waiting for me when I got in, and I've been trying to figure out what it's all about. Been sending some follow-up emails to get more information."

"That sounds ominous."

He backtracks, pasting an encouraging smile on his face, which only makes everything feel more ominous. "Oh no," he says with false lightness, "maybe 'weird' is the wrong word. Unexpected."

I'm not buying it. Despite the smile, or maybe because of it, his whole demeanor seems on edge.

"Maybe it would help to talk about it?" I ask.

"You might be right."

***

I'm sitting at the kitchen table eating buttered toast when Jeremy comes in. Dropping his laptop bag on the sofa, he grabs a soda from the fridge and plops down across from me. "How was your day?" he asks.

I give a somewhat pronounced sigh and say with a wry smile, "Kinda stressful."

With a concerned look, he asks, "What happened?"

"Mark got an email from our supervising organization, and they want to add a fourth person to our team."

"That's a good thing though, isn't it? You've been having some busy days lately. A fourth person might help relieve some of the work strain."

"If it was someone who was the same level as us or someone we selected, I would agree, but apparently this person is going to be above all three of us, and their role is to evaluate all our processes and see where improvements can be made."

"That sounds weird. But you guys are doing awesome, right? I'm sure it'll be fine. Improving what's already going well isn't a bad thing. Maybe they should take it as a compliment that corporate thinks you can handle some new things they're rolling out." Jeremy has always been the positive foil to my pessimistic tendencies.

I raise an eyebrow, unconvinced. "'Weird' is the word Mark used too. Hopefully, you're right. I know I worry about things when I don't need to, but it's hard to not think about how this could be a bad thing. I hope it's actually a positive change."

"You don't need to borrow trouble before it arises, you know."

"From your mouth to God's ears." I huff a laugh. "Sometimes I feel like my mom made a mistake with my middle name being Hazel. 'Worrywart' would've suited me better."

He smiles sympathetically but doesn't laugh at my self-deprecating joke. He never encourages me when I'm hard on myself. "I'm sure things will work out fine," he says reassuringly.

I look at him gratefully.

He pushes his chair back and goes to the pantry. "Do you want me to make you any?" He holds up a can of tomato sauce and a box of penne noodles.

I shake my head and hold up half a piece of toast. "This is the third snack I've had since getting home."

He starts boiling water.

"Did you have a good day today?" I ask a few minutes later, as he dumps the entire box of noodles into the pot.

The noodles rattle and slosh against the pot as he stirs them with a wooden spoon. "It wasn't bad." He gives me a glance. "Yolanda's birthday was today and Stefan brought in a cake, which was nice. We're ramping up on some deadlines but holding steady with progress. Stress levels have seemed manageable for everyone."

"That's always a plus!"

"Yeah, I'm always grateful I work for a company that has their act together and prioritizes work-life balance."

"Same." I feel a twinge as I think about the current situation at The Palette but remind myself that a personnel issue with one individual doesn't negate all the other positive qualities of my job. We'll work through this, I'm sure.

The sauce Jeremy is making smells delicious. I watch him at the stove, alternating between stirring the noodles and the sauce. He has the overhead vent fan on to suck up steam, making conversation impossible.

When he takes the pot to the sink to drain the penne, I jump out of my seat and run to the cupboard to get two bowls.

"Two?" He looks at me incredulously with a twinkle in his eyes. "I knew you couldn't resist my award-winning marinara." He holds up the empty box. "Good thing I made the whole box, Val."

His voice is teasing, and I feel my face flush. I reach for serving spoons and start dishing up pasta. He carries the bowls to the table.

We continue to joke and laugh as we eat, and our interaction feels more companionable than it has in a long time. Some of the tension leaves my shoulders. He's right. I shouldn't borrow trouble before I know things are worth worrying about.

We watch the third and fourth episodes of our new show. After the latter episode ends, Jeremy scrunches down on his side of the sofa. He looks like he's getting ready to fall asleep.

"I'm already seeing what great character development this show has," I say, looking at him.

His eyes are closed, but he nods and says, "Yeah, even the

characters we're not supposed to like. I'm curious what will happen to all of them."

"Do you think the three main characters are heading for a love triangle?"

His eyes open suddenly and he looks at me in shock. "Valancy! Don't jinx it like that. Love triangles are lame!"

I laugh. "They're not lame, Jere. They happen. And I'm not jinxing anything. This show's already well established, so if a love triangle is happening, it's not my fault."

He scoffs and closes his eyes again, crossing his arms comfortably over his chest. "If we end up with a love triangle, I'm blaming you."

"I'm sure you will." I chuckle. "I'm heading to bed. Thanks for the pasta."

"You're welcome. Have a good night."

"You too."

As I head to my side of the house, I think fondly of future evenings consumed with a new show. I'm glad we have an activity to share together again. We've gotten so immersed in our own lives that even though we're roommates and best friends, we haven't spent much time together lately. Combined with the emotional distance, it has made me feel very lonely. It's strange missing someone who's right in front of you.

As I'm brushing my teeth before bed, thoughts of work return. I get into bed with a ripple of worry running along my shoulders.

***

My bedroom's too warm, the darkness too dark, and my mind is racing again in spite of my efforts all evening to redirect my thoughts. Without Jeremy as a sounding board, they play unrestrained in my mind. This change to our gallery could be cataclysmic. It's hard to be rational when it's 1:30 A.M. and I'm lying in a pitch-black room feeling hot and on edge.

I idly stroke Bob where he lies next to me, and he rolls over and gives me his belly. It's a trap I willingly fall for as I focus on the feeling of his soft fur between my fingers for a couple minutes. Okay, I didn't rub his belly for actual minutes—that lasted about ten seconds—but then I petted the rest of him. His contented purrs soothe my frayed nerves. It's good to know I'm not alone in the night. Slowly, my mind calms and my breaths even out.

Wind is rushing past my face. My hair, which is as long, straight, and luscious as I could ever wish, whips into my eyes. I pull it away only to have it immediately get in my eyes again. This happens several times before I start to get aggravated.

A hand gives me a green silk headscarf.

"Here, this will help."

Tying it around my head, I glance at the source of the voice. A woman with waist-length black hair that's miraculously not all over the place is standing next to me at the ship's railing, observing the sea. The sky is perfectly blue and cloudless, and the sun isn't too hot. A few seagulls float on the breeze. It's divine. The movement of the boat doesn't make me feel sick. Instead, we cut through the waves with the wind and spray on my face and arms. It's thrilling. Any chill is melted away by the warm air.

"We'll be docking soon," the woman says.

A picturesque sea village appears in the distance.

"Let's get cappuccinos at a seaside café and share canapes," I say.

"That sounds amazing, but there is somewhere I have to be," she replies wistfully.

The boat lands and I disembark. My floral skirt billows around my strappy gladiator sandals, and a woven belt sits low on my hips. I'm the most glamorous woman in the world.

At the bottom of the gangway, a man in a blue-and-white horizontal-striped shirt takes my hand and winds my arm through his. He has dark, sweeping hair and long sideburns. He cuts a dashing look. The muscles of his arm flex beneath my hand as he leads me along the boardwalk.

"Welcome to paradise! Join me for a root beer float." He gestures up ahead.

The sun is warm on my face as I allow him to lead me to the most charming sidewalk establishment. It's complete with cobblestones, plant boxes, tables with pairs of chairs, and red-and-white umbrellas.

The waitress, who looks remarkably similar to the woman from the boat, brings out our floats. I thank her and she meows in response.

The dream slips away as Bob meows in my face again. I pet him a few times, roll over, and find a cool spot on my pillow.

***

I'm heading up a packed escalator. Leaning as far over as I can to avoid touching the person next to me, I'm careful to not bump those in front and behind. I see playground-style slides for people who are heading down. Lucky them. The escalator deposits me at the top and I try to get on the next big one going up, but I get jostled onto a different up one. This one is narrow, with no room beside me. That's a relief until I notice I'm the only one on this escalator and the fluorescent lighting is dimming and flickering. When the light fully snuffs out, there is a moment of mounting panic before suddenly I'm on the roof outside. It's sunset. The return of any light, particularly the subtle warmth of natural light, instantly calms me. The stuffy, claustrophobic air is replaced by sweet-smelling freshness.

I'm deposited in a grassy community space. I'm near a playground, the wooden kind that were amazing in the 1990s and now are all but a memory. In the distance is a huge Ferris wheel and the biggest swing ride I've ever seen. It has ten layers of swings, some spinning counterclockwise. Between the rides and the park is a patchwork city of mismatched buildings. There are standard tenements butting up against opulent museums, sidewalk cafés with purple awnings, and shady dive bars, and there is even a Victorian mansion next to a red-and-yellow fast-food joint.

The view leaves me awestruck for a minute, there's so much to look at. Suddenly, the people are back in droves, and I'm jostled every which way. I'm spun around and the fast-food place whirls by, then the playground, then purple awnings. I close my eyes to shut out the onslaught.

"Hey, are you all right?"

I cautiously open my eyes and find myself sitting against an aspen tree in a quiet part of the park. The hordes are gone, and children are playing nearby as their grownups watch. No one glances my way. The source of the voice is a man sitting cross-legged next to me.

"Y-yes." I fumble for words; my head is still swirling. "There were too many people." I'm not sure what else to say.

"Yeah, that happens. C'mon, let's get you a treat." He grasps my hand and leads me to the dingiest of the dingy dive bars. It has a picture of a pickle with a floral top hat on the sign. The interior is pink and white stripes. A girl in a short, yellow dress with a ruffled petticoat brings me an enormous banana split. And when I say enormous, I mean I must look around it to see the man sitting across from me.

I stare at him for a moment. He has brown wavy hair that I'm sure he regularly runs his hands through—the kind every woman wishes she had, but some man ended up with it—and dark hazel eyes.

He laughs. "Is everything okay? You going to eat that?"

I glance back at my dessert, but it's not appetizing anymore; the whipped cream and cherry are sagging to one side. I look back up at him, but he has transformed into Bob sitting on my chest, staring at me with narrowed eyes.

It takes me a moment to get my bearings. Despite their implausibility, my dreams often feel real, and the line between them and reality can be blurry for a moment or two after waking up. I don't remember a time when I had normal dream habits.

A pair of hazel eyes with a quirked eyebrow still gazes expectantly at me. Not Bob's, his are yellow. Maybe if I don't move much, I can drift off and continue the dream as I've occasionally been able to do in the past. I fight consciousness. Bob butts me firmly with his head. I reach out a hand to stroke him and resist the urge to roll over. No such luck, the real world resolutely reels me in and Bob playfully sinks his teeth into my fingers, just hard enough to get me moving. After tossing and turning for a few minutes, while giving Bob some more pets, I drift off again.

Chapter 3

I'm tired today; last night wasn't restful. I'm annoyed with Bob for being needy and with my room for being uncomfortable. The real cause of my tempestuous sleep was stress, but it's so much easier to blame the cat for my problems than myself.

I'm not in the best of moods when I get to work, but the peace of The Palette before opening helps me relax. We're not doing our morning snack today because Mark is at a meeting of local galleries. It's only Daphne and me holding down the fort this morning.

"How's Fred feeling today?" I ask as we move around the Main Gallery, tidying displays before opening.

She chuckles fondly. "Little ones are so resilient, you know? He gets stuck like a pin cushion yesterday and today you'd never know that anything was amiss."

"I wish it was like that for me. The flu shot takes me down for at least a full day, and don't get me started on the more serious vaccines."

"I feel ya. Literally. That's me and Esteban too. We have to time vaccinations for ourselves on different days, otherwise Fred might be left to his own devices." She winks. "I'm kidding, of course."

I already knew that.

Daphne is stationed at the front desk for the first half of the day while I wander around the galleries, tidying up and helping patrons. We've had a steady flow of visitors thus far this morning.

"Excuse me, miss, could you help me with this?" a young woman calls out to me as I'm passing through the Main Gallery to go chat with Daphne for a minute.

"Of course," I respond pleasantly, heading over to the wall of artworks that the woman is standing in front of. "What do you need help with?"

"See that purple landscape with the orange pickup truck?" She points to a painting that's high on the wall. "I want to buy that."

"Oh, that's got itself a little ways up there, hasn't it? Let me go get the step ladder, I'll be right back." It takes me a minute to locate the ladder and drag it to the front of the gallery. By the time I get back, the customer has circled farther around the jewelry island and is admiring a display of paper mâché hot air balloon mobiles. She's leaning over to get a better look at one when I walk up, hefting the step ladder awkwardly.

She straightens and smiles at me. "You have such a cool assortment of artworks for sale here. Haven't I seen these hot air balloons before somewhere?"

"Quite likely. The artist who makes those, Peggy Leonard, got featured on the local news a couple years ago and ended up going viral. We're super lucky that she chooses to continue keeping a supply of her pieces here at The Paint Palette. Folks still get excited when they see them for sale in the wild. I think we probably owe her patronage to being a long-time family friend of my boss's parents."

"Whatever the reason, I think she's lucky to be part of such a vibrant art organization. If I were an artist, I'd want to have my art up here." She looks around appreciatively.

It warms my heart when people say nice things about The Palette.

We move back in the direction of the artwork she wants to buy. I set up the ladder and pull the frame down, handing it to her. She thanks me, looks around a bit more, and heads up front to check out with Daphne.

The week continues uneventfully. There is an undercurrent of worry since we haven't heard from Mark's boss with any follow-up information about the new person for our team, but we're all actively trying to stay optimistic. Daphne has been working on programming for a ladies' group event that's coming up, and Mark is sorting through financial paperwork in preparation for the upcoming tax season, which leaves me to handle the swapping out of Cottontail from a pottery display to the new quarterly exhibit featuring Mr. Howard's work.

Our current pottery exhibit, which has an overarching theme of floral toasters with mice, has been particularly popular. The artist, Emma Galaxy, is from the next town over, where the Renaissance Fair currently is, and she's tickled about how many of her pieces sold. She had to restock at one point because her allocated space was getting sparse. It's Thursday. She and I are bubble wrapping her remaining pieces as we move her show out in preparation for the next one.

Next Friday, Bryce Hampton will be bringing in some of his huge abstract paintings and other items for his show. He has shown here before, and his pieces are more typical for our gallery, but he didn't have many sales last time. We think he priced things too high for the demographics of this area; we're a small town, after all. He's going to implement some of our recommendations this time.

His opening reception will be on a Saturday two weeks after he sets up. Saturday is normally my day off, but I'll come in for a few hours in the evening. He and I will discuss the details for the event when he comes in next week. That way, I can plan a reception that works with his vision. I've already got the social media posts, mailers, signage, and posters ready to go, but we'll work out the kinds of refreshments, music, decorations, and such.

"Valancy," Ms. Galaxy says slowly as she places a bubble wrapped parcel in a box. "What is the story behind your name? I don't think I've ever heard of anyone with it before."

"My mother had an author she loved as a teen, and the main character in her favorite book was named Valancy. After reading that book, she vowed to herself that if she ever had a daughter, that's what she'd name her."

"I love that! I'm also named for a character in a book!" I assume she's referring to Emma, since I know she picked Galaxy out for herself. She looks proud. I know how she feels. I've always loved my name's origin story. We talk more about the characters we were named after. When we exhaust this topic, conversation lags as we're consumed with our work.

A couple minutes later, Ms. Galaxy asks, "Who's the next show in here?"

"Bryce Hampton. He had a show here a year and a half ago. He's the one with the huge abstract canvases that sort of resemble fruit."

"Oh yes, I think I came to his reception. I didn't talk to him, just enjoyed the show and refreshments. He creates beautiful pieces, but a bit on the expensive side." She says the last bit in a stage whisper. "But he's a real dreamboat, so maybe I'll come again and work up the courage to talk to him this time."

I chuckle. "Yes, he was disappointed with his sales last time. We recommended some adjustments, and he's modified his ideas for this show. He should have a balance with smaller and less expensive options this time around. And he is very nice; I'm sure he'd love to meet you."

"Additional incentive! I have a few open spaces on my walls that might work for the style of art he makes."

I smile to myself, pleased that our ideas for improvements are already increasing interest.

We're almost done when Mark leans around the archway.

"You ladies doing good in here?" He looks around nostalgically. "It's always sad when a show comes down. You'll have to come back and do a show with us again, Ms. Galaxy." He grins widely at her.

"It's been a blast to be able to do this, Mr. Abede. It has fueled my self-esteem that folks have gotten excited about what I make." She beams at him.

"I'm glad we're able to offer this. Valancy, when you're done helping Ms. Galaxy, could you pop back to my desk?"

"Sure thing, Mark. We'll probably be another ten minutes or so."

"No rush!" His voice floats in from the Main Gallery. He's already off about other matters.

Ms. Galaxy has left the building, although I see her talking to Elton out front, so she may be here for a few more minutes.

I head back to the office area. Mark is clicking away at something on his screen.

"Hey, what's up?" I sit down in the chair adjacent to his desk.

He looks up, taking a moment to focus. "Oh hey, thanks for reminding me. I wanted to tell you that the new person will be coming in sometime next week. I didn't get a clear answer about exactly when."

"No worries. We should be able to manage a random arrival. We won't be in the middle of anything next week, and none of us will be on vacation."

He nods. "That's what I thought too. We'll clean off the desk in the corner for them to use. Would you mind taking care of that? You have a nice feel for the esthetic; I know you'll make it feel welcoming."

"Of course! I love doing stuff like that." He looks grateful. "Have you heard any more about what they'll be doing?"

"A couple emails that have made it sound very straightforward. I think I might have freaked out about everything prematurely."

I pat his shoulder as I feel some of the tightness I've been holding leave mine. "That's okay, it's understandable. We've gotten comfortable with our routine, and it was sudden. Change can be hard to adjust to, particularly if those delivering it aren't conscientious about the best method for delivery." I always sound so reasonable after a crisis has been averted.

"My thoughts exactly. Some of those corporate emails can sound harsh until you understand what the motivation was behind them." He glances at his computer but then seems to shake himself mentally and turns back to me. "Since Ms. Galaxy is all done and Thursdays are our slowest day, what do you say to you, me, and Daphne turning the sign to 'Closed' and going out to lunch? There's a new taco shop on Cicada Street that I keep hearing about."

"That sounds amazing! I'm sure Daphne will think so too."

***

"Would you like to go to that new Tortilla de Maiz place for lunch or dinner sometime? Mark took us there today and they had big portions, and everything was super flavorful and juicy." I'm annoyed with myself for feeling nervous in anticipation of Jeremy's response. This is a very reasonable suggestion, and I shouldn't feel apprehensive. It's just that I still don't know how to navigate our current dynamic.

I'm leaning in the doorway of the kitchen, trying to appear nonchalant, which I'm not sure is working. I have this fantastic capacity for awkwardness. My casual stance and crossed arms may actually be conveying discomfort.

Jeremy doesn't look up from smearing peanut butter on some toast. I watch him closely, and I think I see his shoulders stiffen a bit and then forcibly relax. He takes a long breath before he looks over at me. "That sounds good. The cashier at the grocery store was telling me about that place, and I've been wanting to try it." He flushes a bit and adds, "It'd be nice to go with you." He flashes a quick smile and turns hurriedly back to his lunch preparation. His ears are pinker than normal.

"Great!" I exclaim with more pep than is warranted and head back to my room. I was going to make myself something to eat, but now my insides feel all messed up, and the sanctuary of my room feels safer than the charged air around Jeremy.

I don't know what has happened lately. Okay, actually I do know—with me, at least—but it's all awkward and uncomfortable and speculative, which is why I'm not taking steps to confront him.

Let me back up.

I mentioned before that Jeremy and I had a thing in college our junior year. A more accurate statement would be that I had a massive crush on Jeremy while he was dating someone else. I can feel you rolling your eyes. Stop that. I didn't *do* anything about it. I didn't tell him or try to sabotage his relationship with Natalie in any way. Satisfied? I just felt what I felt, which I couldn't help. I refuse to apologize for feelings. Actions, yes. Feelings are just something that happen.

It threw me for a loop because in the ten years that we'd been friends, I'd never had feelings for him before. I'd dated some losers and he'd dated some divas, and it never seriously affected our friendship. We teased each other mercilessly whenever the other was wrapped up in a fling, but it never changed how we felt about each other.

Not until Natalie.

Natalie was different. She was nice. That's not as petty as

it sounds. What I'm trying to say is that Natalie was the first person who really had the possibility of coming between us. Not because she would've tried to stop us from being friends; she wouldn't have, but because there was the real possibility I might get replaced. Not that anyone would've done that deliberately, but you know how these things can happen. Boy meets girl and they become best friends. Then boy meets other girl and falls in love and never sees female friend again. A story as old as time.

Giving Jeremy full credit, this was a Valancy issue, not a him or even a Natalie issue. Jeremy dating Natalie made me realize everything I'd been ignoring. All the potential of what I could lose engulfed me.

Sparing you the dramatic details, let me just say that I could've conducted myself better. I didn't try to break them up, but I definitely didn't get a gold star for being a good friend either. But who wants a gold star when your world just got flipped upside down?

As opposed to confronting my feelings head on and admitting I'd loved Jeremy all my life, I decided to bottle everything up and pretend it didn't exist. Definitely the healthy route. Clearly, I'm aware of those feelings now, but I've had over a decade to come to terms with immature me and figure out how to not dwell on that.

At the time, I isolated myself from Jeremy, left him and Natalie to their romantic bubble, and threw myself into my art classes. I didn't ghost him, but I significantly reduced contact, delayed responding, and generally allowed our friendship to drift. I know it hurt his feelings and that he didn't understand what had changed. Or maybe he did but didn't know how to talk about it. I guess it wouldn't have taken a rocket scientist, after all. But Jeremy is only a computer scientist. Did he make the connection between his relationship with Natalie and the sudden cooling of our friendship?

Jeremy and Natalie dated for the rest of college, and I waited with bated breath for the ax of "We're engaged!" to fall, but it never did. I don't know exactly what happened, but after college they went their separate ways. She was a journalism major, and when she got a good job offer in New York City, she took it. He stayed here.

Our friendship didn't heal overnight. We started our careers and pursued our own interests, but I think being in the real world was an eye-opener. We'd grown up together and experienced the growing pains of life jointly. It was inevitable that when the rude awakening of adulthood happened, we would turn to each other for support.

Of course, the new version of our friendship wasn't the same as it had been before Natalie. My feelings were firmly locked up with the key thrown away, and the things I should have told him remained unsaid. But our friendship healed and we became good friends again, and I'm forever grateful that we had that second chance.

We've been roommates for about five years now, and it has been the best. We're well suited to cohabitate, and we don't get on each other's nerves. It's also a plus that Jeremy is very fond of Bob. It would have been a deal breaker if he hated cats.

Let me fast forward to today.

Do I still have feelings for Jeremy? I suppose so, but I've learned to live with them. I'm not bottling them up anymore. I'm proud of myself for that. I've tried dating other people, but no one has felt worth the effort. I've accepted my current single state with minimal bitterness.

Why have I never told him about my feelings? Mostly because I'm afraid of the consequences. I value his friendship too much to risk it all for the brief satisfaction of finally airing my inner thoughts.

So, what's going on with Jeremy? To be honest, that's the part I find confusing too. We've both dated other people off and on over the years, people I would say have been generally nice and not the divas or losers of our younger years. He hasn't dated anyone in a while, and in the past several months he has become more closed off and avoidant with me. I can feel you giving me an all-knowing look, so let me tell you, I've considered that he might have feelings for me. But I've also known him for twenty-five years through all manner of upheavals and life events and although him suddenly being in love with me is a possibility, there are also, like, forty-two other possible options, which I won't list here in the interest of not boring you to death.

That one possibility is what's causing my mental chaos around him lately, though.

Chapter 4

VALANCY

About a week later, I'm up front after lunch. Prep of Cottontail is complete and ready for Bryce's arrival tomorrow, and our new staff member's desk has been cleaned and welcomingly decorated. I decided to treat myself to lunch out for a change. My brother works down the street at an autobody shop, and he was able to get off at the same time. We met up at a new salad place, my choice—he picked last time. Tanner isn't the biggest fan of salads, but he'll tolerate one here and there for my benefit as long as I get wings with him when it's his turn to pick. We never connected well as kids, maybe because of our age gap, but I do love knowing he's nearby if I ever need him.

Jeremy and I are going to meet at Tortillas de Maiz after I get off work. I'm looking forward to it. It sounds kind of cheesy to dress up for dinner with someone I live with and see every day, but I did put on a figure-hugging green blouse with long bishop sleeves to be a teeny bit fancier than my norm. I don't want it to seem like I dressed up for tacos, but a little extra effort feels good. Green also complements my red hair.

I check to see if any new emails have come through in the last hour. Once I'm satisfied that nothing urgent has appeared, I get up and start straightening some of the displays closer to the desk. The bells over the door tinkle and I glance up as Ms. Galaxy sashays in. I wish I had half her natural grace.

"Hey, Ms. Galaxy, it's nice to see you!" I straighten a final item and walk over to greet her.

She smiles brightly as I approach and says, "I'm glad it's you at the desk, Valancy. You're the one I wanted to see. I brought this for you." She holds out a parcel for me. I take it and she motions for me to open it. Inside is one of her little toaster statues, a figurine of a tiny mouse peeking around the side of a blue toaster, holding a buttercup in its paw. It's adorable. I look at her, confused.

"It's for you," she says. "I've been thinking about it, and I want you to have it because you put so much effort and time into my show. It's a token of my appreciation. I thought this might work since you seem to appreciate my pieces."

I'm touched. "Thank you, Ms. Galaxy." I run my finger over the mouse's sleek ceramic back. "It was such a pleasure working with you and helping your show to be a success. I do love it, thank you." I set the figurine on the counter, where I won't forget it.

Suddenly, a voice from the hallway leading to our office area exclaims sharply, "Did you pay for that?"

My spine stiffens and my head snaps toward the unfamiliar and accusing voice. A tall beanpole of a man is standing in the doorway. His thinning hair and argyle sweater vest remind me of my uncle Ned, who is a professor of anthropology. I begin to stammer, because he has caught me completely off guard. I didn't realize anyone besides Mark and Daphne was here. My mouth opens and closes a couple times like a goldfish; this isn't my finest moment.

Fortunately, Ms. Galaxy takes the situation in hand.

"No, she most certainly did not *pay for it*. It was a gift from me to her," she says, her hand with its wrist tinkling with bangles propped saucily on her hip. She's having none of his tone.

I blink at her and look back at him, wondering how he'll respond.

"Since it's an item in our gallery, it should be paid for. Otherwise, we don't get the commission for it," he responds sternly.

I look back at Ms. Galaxy. How will she parry? Also, what's this about "our gallery"? Who is this guy?

"My contract with you ended last week. My show is all packed up and gone, and I brought this piece back to Valancy from *my house*. None of my items are for sale with you today, which means I am free to do with them as I please." She sniffs disdainfully and turns away from him, clearly done explaining, and says to me sweetly and pointedly, "Thank *you* again, Valancy. I hope you enjoy it. I'll be in touch." She rolls her eyes so only I can see, smiles quickly, turns intentionally to not face the beanpole as she leaves, and breezes out the door without a second glance.

The bells tinkle again on her way out, sounding discordantly cheerful compared to the current mood she has left behind.

As the melodious sound fades and heavy silence descends, I take a breath and turn toward the unpleasant interloper. He's still standing in the same place, but he looks angry, and his arms are crossed. I can't see his feet, but I wouldn't be surprised if he's also tapping his foot.

He opens his mouth, and I feel myself flinch now that his ire is going to be directed fully at me. Fortunately, Mark appears at the moment and interrupts the situation.

"Valancy!" he exclaims with forced cheerfulness. "You're back from lunch! *Wonderful.* I see you've met Clarance. He's the new teammate I said would be coming soon! Clarance, this is Valancy. She manages our rotating shows and helps with sales and marketing. She's awesome!" Mark's face is all buoyant brightness and false exuberance. His uneasiness and worry are palpable. He looks expectantly between the two of us, hoping we'll take his cheery, exclamation-pointed bait.

There is silence for a beat. Then another.

Finally, since Clarance seems unwilling to extend any olive

branch in this encounter, I walk over and extend my hand to him. "It's nice to meet you properly. I hope you'll love working here with us. We have a lot of fun." I smile perfunctorily.

He's clearly unimpressed. He doesn't return my smile, but he does reach for my hand and weakly shakes it. Ugh! Worst handshake ever! I drop it as quickly as politeness allows.

"I'm not here to have fun. I'm here to make a difference," says Clarance grumpily.

Now it's Mark's turn to look back and forth between us. He gazes at me to see how I'll respond.

I stare at Clarance levelly. "I don't think they're mutually exclusive. I believe we make a difference in the lives of our artists every day." I turn away and head down the hall.

I hear Mark making strained small talk, likely glad our meeting didn't go any worse. I doubt that Clarance is the type for idle chatting; best of luck to Mark.

Back in our desk area, Daphne is eating cucumber slices while typing up an email. I carefully close the door and lean against it with a huff, resting my head against the wood. Her eyes glance at me over the top of the computer screen. "You met Clarance." It's not a question.

"I would say 'unfortunately' except I know it's his first day, and I'd prefer to give him the benefit of the doubt. Give me a minute to convince myself that's a good idea."

She quirks an eyebrow. "I'm not sure he deserves that consideration."

"Maybe not, but if it was me and I wasn't presenting as my best self in a new place, I would want a little grace. However, if he's still awful this time next week, I'll revise my assessment accordingly." I laugh ruefully. "He's definitely not making the best first impression."

She shakes her head in agreement.

I sit down at my desk and pull up an old file I've been working on at odd moments when I have free time. It's something to do until Clarance leaves the Main Gallery area. I'm going to let Mark figure out the front desk. I know he'll understand.

After a few minutes with no interruptions, I take a deep breath and push my shoulders down, forcing myself to relax. My first encounter with Clarance wasn't promising, but I try to put it as far from the front of my thoughts as possible to not ruin my mood too much. As I said to Daphne, I do believe he deserves a chance to settle in before he's judged too harshly.

The rest of the day is spent comparatively uneventfully. Mark trains Clarance on front desk operations, and Daphne and I work at our desks in the back. Fortunately, there's no need to interact further with Clarance. When we leave for the day, his goodbye is terse but reasonably polite. I feel a small spark of hope.

***

My enthusiasm for dinner has been dampened by the end of the day, but I check my appearance in my car's mirror before getting out. Still looking cute. I pull my long ponytail over my shoulder and smooth it a bit with my hands. Then I catch myself, roll my eyes, and flip it back over my shoulder. *Get it together, Val, it's just tacos with Jeremy.*

Jeremy has already got a booth at the right when I walk in. He came directly from work and is still wearing his work clothes. His black polo flatters his medium skin tone. It's a little tight and hugs his biceps and chest, and a tattoo of an amphibian he got after graduation peeks out of his sleeve. My breath hitches a tiny bit. *Pathetic, Valancy.*

I sit down across from him. His initial welcoming smile changes to a look of concern. "Is everything okay?" he asks, his forehead furrowed.

I must not be hiding it well. "The new guy started."

"Oh boy, not good?"

I sigh audibly. "I told Daphne I'm going to give him a chance, but he made a lousy first impression. I'm worried."

"That sucks. Do you want to order and then we can talk about it?" He gestures to the counter.

"Okay." I make myself smile. As always, I'm glad to spend time with Jeremy, and I appreciate that he never dismisses me. We walk up to the counter together.

"What'd you order last time?" He leans toward me while looking up at the hanging menu. I catch a whiff of his cologne. It's a good smell that I've always liked. Fortunate, since our house smells like it regularly.

"I got the *carne asada* street tacos."

He nods, considering his options.

"Daphne got the *pollo* and Mark got *carnitas*. We all loved what we ordered. Seems like you can't go wrong here."

The attendant comes to the register and takes Jeremy's order. He gets the *carne asada* tacos. I wait for her to ring him up, but he gestures for me to order. "What do you want, Val?"

I'm caught off guard. Aside for occasional convenience purchases, we don't usually pay for each other.

"Oh, um, I'll have the same thing. And a soda, please. Thank you." I wait while he pays and then take our cups to the machine.

When I return to the table, Jeremy picks up our previous conversation. "Tell me about the new guy."

I consider what to say as I remove my straw from the wrapper. Thoughts of Clarance make my insides writhe. "Ugh. Someone came in on a personal errand, and he inserted himself into the conversation in the most obnoxious way. He was rude and full of condemnation, and you could tell it upset the visitor. This was all before we'd been introduced. He didn't have to be nasty, but he was. None of us were doing anything wrong, but the way he approached everything made us feel as though our teacher caught us eating worms."

Jeremy raises an eyebrow and seems to restrain a smile at my metaphor. "Maybe he handles change badly and this is putting him out of his element."

"That's what I was thinking too, but somebody should've given him some pointers on how to behave on your first day at a new workplace. Attack dog mode isn't the way."

"It's possible that he read that misconception about managers needing to start their relationships with subordinates firmly. That way, they don't get walked all over."

"Subordinates," I scoff. "There are only three of us. It works much better in small situations like ours to treat everyone equally, while acknowledging that some employees may have additional responsibilities."

"You know that, and I know that, but maybe this... what's his name?"

"Clarance."

"...Clarance doesn't know. Maybe he needs some time to figure things out. Just because he's an adult in an elevated position doesn't mean he's self-aware or bursting with people skills."

"That he most certainly is not. I hope he becomes more agreeable soon. We already weren't pleased with how this situation was handled, but we never would've let that affect how we treated him. If he keeps behaving in this manner, he's going to find that we have buttons that can get pushed too many times and limits to our goodwill."

Our baskets of tacos arrive with complementing sides of green chile, onions, salsa, and beans. Everything smells amazing. We dig in, and I giggle with delight when Jeremy groans with pleasure.

"You weren't kidding that the food here is good," he gushes.

"When have I ever been wrong?" I ask, mock offended.

He snickers, his mouth full, and grins at me. "I'll never doubt you again."

"I'll believe that when I see it, or rather, when I don't."

Our conversation shifts to lighter topics, and I feel myself relaxing and enjoying our dinner. I'm glad he agrees that I should give Clarance some leeway as he adjusts to his new role.

As I'm drifting off to sleep tonight, I think about talking with Jeremy. Mostly it makes me smile, except for the part about Clarance. I want him to be a reasonable person to work with, but I'm worried he won't end up living up to my hopes. I mentally shake myself. *Enough of that, Valancy, worrying won't resolve anything. Think of sunshine and butterflies and try to sleep.* I laugh at myself but do actively try to change the direction of my thoughts to something less agitating.

Chapter 5

VALANCY

Heading up a narrow escalator, I start to panic because I realize I'm alone and it's getting progressively darker. Just as I'm about to freak out, suddenly I'm standing in a grassy park with sunlight slanting through trees, staring at a hodgepodge skyline of mismatched buildings.

"Well, this is a first for me. I've never heard of anyone coming back," a voice says behind me.

When I turn, I'm face to face with an attractive, hazel-eyed man with brown hair. "What did you say?" My voice sounds breathless.

He looks at me oddly. "Never mind. Is something wrong?" He smiles kindly, straightening his shoulders slightly.

"I'm fine." I look away from him. His gaze is penetrating, making me feel uneasy, but he doesn't need to know that.

Chuckling, and clearly unperturbed, he says, "Let's go

get you a treat," before taking my hand and pulling me in the direction of a sketchy bar.

I yank back on his hand.

He doesn't let go, but he stops and turns to me, raising an eyebrow questioningly.

"Why do you think I need a treat?" I ask.

He thinks about this a moment, then shrugs. "Why wouldn't you need a treat?"

There's no arguing with that. I stop resisting and allow him to drag me along.

I release a breath I didn't realize I was holding when we walk inside and I see high tops with green leather chairs and soccer playing on the televisions over the bar.

My companion chuckles again. "Not the décor you were expecting?"

My look is sharp. "What do you mean?" This guy is starting to get on my nerves with his cryptic comments.

Gathering himself, he smiles disarmingly, holding his hands out placatingly. "Never mind. Please, forget I said anything." He pulls out my chair for me, indicating for me to sit.

I open my mouth to retort, not inclined to let him subdue my curiosity, but the waitress comes up to us at that moment. She has a green apron with long ties wrapped around her waist. Her black T-shirt and jeans sport some flour spots. The largest stack of onion rings you've ever seen is placed in front of me. I lean around it to see the man sitting across from me.

I inspect him intently for a moment. His hair is wavy and shoulder length, and I'm jealous on behalf of all the women who look at a man and roll their eyes that he's the one who ended up with such hair. He's looking at me in amusement. It's hard to tell at this distance in the dim light, but I bet he has killer eyelashes.

Inexplicably, he laughs. "Is everything okay? You going to eat that?"

I look at my onion rings, then back up at him as he watches me expectantly. I take a bite and gesture to the stack. "Do you want one?" I can try to play nice.

He chuckles again. His unending amusement at my expense is starting to get on my nerves. As he crunches into an onion ring, he exclaims, "Oh, these aren't bad! Good job!"

Clearly, it makes more sense to ignore this guy than engage with him. Angling my body away from him, I inspect my surroundings. Golden light filters in from the back windows, and I see a swing ride spinning in the distance. Dust motes catch the sun and sparkle as they settle. The green décor with the gilded light has a magical quality.

My attention is dragged back to the man across from me. The light is catching his hair and the sides of his irises, giving him an almost ethereal glow. He isn't the handsomest, but this ambiance lends itself to him, and it takes my breath away for a moment.

"*Is* everything okay?" he asks. For once, there's no humor in his voice.

Nodding, I notice his eyes looking at me admiringly. His fingers twitch, and he looks away quickly. The waitress comes up to see how we're doing.

She says, "*BEEP-BEEP-BEEP.*"

I'm spread-eagled in my bed. My alarm blares a few more times before I reach over sleepily and turn it off. I fall back against my pillows, staring at the ceiling. After a couple minutes, I get out of bed and start going through the motions of getting ready for work. My mind is still halfway in my dream. I'm confused about what happened.

I've had this dream before, sort of. I recognize it now that I'm awake. I also met that man before in the same dream. I've had repeat or continuation dreams before, but those only happened when I specially focused my mind on them to bring them about. I didn't do that with this one. Until this dream happened last night, I had no memory of the prior one.

About halfway through my morning tea, I start to feel my normal, real-world self returning, and dread for the coming workday settles on my shoulders like a mantle.

Chapter 6

VALANCY

I'm pleased to see I'm running earlier than usual to work this morning despite the rough wake-up and my stop to pick up breakfast treats. I'll have some time alone at the gallery before Daphne and Mark... and Clarance... arrive. I can tidy the kitchen and set out the blueberry muffins I picked up. There may have been some mental pats on the back for myself when I bought one for Clarance too. I've decided I'm going to give this an A+ effort. Or at least a B+; I never was a straight-A student.

Turning into The Palette's parking lot, I'm dismayed to see Clarance's white SUV already there. It hadn't occurred to me that he might be an early bird. My enthusiasm diminished, I head inside. Clarance is already at the front desk, which has been tidied to within an inch of its life. He has a can of tomato juice popped open and a protein bar with the wrapper neatly folded back sitting on a napkin placed in front of him.

Think happy thoughts, Valancy. We're going to give this a B+ effort, I remind myself. "Good morning," I say cheerfully, trying to smile as genuinely as possible. I'm pleased when I hear a melodious tone issue from my mouth.

"Hello." He barely glances up and goes back to perusing the document in front of him. At least he wasn't outright rude, I guess.

I take a steadying breath. "I brought in blueberry muffins." I hold up the box. "Normally, we sit on the patio together to start our day. I can start some coffee or tea for you, or you can bring your… juice…." My voice trails off, but I still smile expectantly. The effort makes my cheeks feel taut.

He looks up at me and says, deadpan, "I don't have time to waste being idle." He looks back down at his papers, clearly dismissing me. "And I hate blueberries," he throws out as an afterthought jab.

I feel myself bristling with indignation. In an attempt to hold back my feelings, I respond simply with a forced, "Suit yourself." My tone is no longer musical, but it doesn't sound rude either. *Neutral is fine*, I assure myself. *B+ efforts don't need to be musical.*

"I will, thanks." He doesn't look up, so he doesn't see my face turning red. I can feel the heat rising on my skin. I wish my emotions hid themselves better. Even when I can disguise my tone, I tend to blush when I have strong feelings. I turn on my heel and unceremoniously dump the blueberry muffin box in the kitchenette. So much for trying to include him and being pleasant. He's insufferable!

My face is still hot, and my breaths are pumping out in short pants. I take a couple deeper breaths to calm myself. Once they even out and my face feels cool again, I head to my desk.

The rest of the day doesn't go any better.

Daphne and Mark come in at the same time. I hear muffled conversation from up front and assume they aren't faring any better than me. When they get back to their desks, they're clearly on edge, frowns firmly in place. Greetings between us are terse, and by unspoken agreement, we forego our morning routine and have our muffins and drinks at our desks without conversation. The only thing I'm excited for today is Mr. Hampton's gallery setup.

Around 11:15, Bryce and I are in the middle of hanging his exhibit in Cottontail when Clarance comes into the small gallery.

"Are you really going to hang that piece there?" he asks disparagingly.

Bryce and I crane our necks toward him. We're in the progress of lifting a large canvas for placement on the wall, and have hold of opposite sides. We lower it to a more comfortable position. Fleetingly, I consider letting Mr. Hampton respond, but no, this is my responsibility.

"There isn't anywhere else to put it, Clarance. It's the largest of Mr. Hampton's pieces, and we tried it on the other wall that doesn't have a doorway, but it doesn't look right," I respond professionally. I don't want Bryce knowing there's workplace tension.

Clarance huffs. "Well, I suppose if there is nowhere else for it." He's gone as quickly as he appeared.

Bryce looks at me questioningly, and I smile as though nothing is wrong. "Let's try that again," I say brightly. We heft the canvas back up and secure it to the wall. I look around at his other items for the show. He has done an excellent job of diversifying his offerings for this exhibit and Cottontail looks quite engaging, with different display areas for smaller pieces and prints and the large signature canvases setting the tone for the entire space. After I admire it all for a moment, I look over at Bryce to see his reaction.

"What do you think?" I ask.

He looks delighted. "It's wonderful! I'm pleased with your suggestions and how this all came together." He smiles happily at me. "Now, you had some final details for the reception you wanted to go over?"

I nod and open my mouth to respond, when Clarance appears again, this time with a clipboard. His timing is too perfect; has he been lurking? He smiles broadly, which is a disconcerting sight since I didn't know he could smile, and says, "Actually, *I* have some suggestions."

I gape at him as Bryce turns to him politely.

Clarance immediately jumps in with a deluge of ideas completely different from anything we've ever done before. For a minute, I consider trying to get back control of the conversation, but clearly Clarance knows he has a fingerhold and he isn't going to let go easily. Giving up, I head to the front desk, feeling disappointed and defeated. I'm sad this reception is getting taken away from me. Planning receptions is one of my favorite things to do at work. Hopefully, Bryce won't be disappointed.

Bryce and Clarance are absorbed in their discussion for the next fifteen minutes. I begrudgingly sit at the front desk while they talk. As he's leaving, Bryce stops by, smiling. "Hey, that new guy is incredibly passionate! I always thought receptions had to be boring hors d'oeuvres and awkward standing around. I'm looking forward to this event!"

I blink in shock before I pull myself together. "That's great! I'm sure it'll be a wonderful," I say positively, pasting a smile on my face.

He smiles and waves and heads out the door, leaving me feeling off kilter and confused.

In the afternoon, I walk into the Main Gallery and find Clarance perusing displays with a clipboard in his hands. He's making tiny marks and Xs on a spreadsheet. He's here to make improvements, I suppose. Helpfully, I ask, "Taking a look around? Let me know if you have any questions. We have many great artists and—"

"I'm good." He cuts me off, not looking up from his clipboard.

I'm left gaping like a fish again, feeling foolish. Again. "Okay, if you're sure. I know—"

"I said, I'm good. I don't need your assistance." He looks up at me, irritation lacing his words and crossing his face.

"Sorry to bother you." I'm shocked at his rudeness. I know he didn't ask for help, but he's new here, and I can tell him valuable information about our business and artists that isn't found on the displays. Whatever he's working on, surely it would be helpful to have insight from long-standing employees. But then again, maybe not. How can I know when he has shut down every positive advance? I turn on my heel and head back to my desk.

***

Jeremy knocks on the door and leans into my room. "How was the second day with the new guy?" he asks.

I'm curled up in my armchair, playing on my phone. "It was stressful. I took your advice and made a big effort, but Clarance didn't end up being any better today. I think maybe he was worse." I look up at him dolefully. Jeremy looks troubled. I quickly add, "Nothing truly horrible. He's just unpleasant and rude. I think it's mostly that I'm mourning our dynamic that he's shattered. I haven't been able to figure out how to communicate with him effectively or reach him with kindness. He's always got a negative comeback to any positive overture from any of us. He responds the most respectfully to Mark, probably because Mark is the highest ranked, but he certainly isn't pleasant. It seems like he dislikes me in particular."

Jeremy murmurs sympathetically.

"It's fine, just discouraging. I was excited to plan Mr. Hampton's reception, and Clarance steamrolled in and took over. At least Mr. Hampton seems happy about it."

Jeremy nods, leaning against my doorframe. "It sounds as though he's a real grouch, but if anyone can reach him, it'll be you. Maybe he's deliberately resisting you most because he sees the effort you're making to connect with him. As you get to know him better, I bet you gain more insight into why he behaves in this way."

"That's such a contrary way to behave, though!" I whine, looking dramatically at the ceiling. "It's hard for me to comprehend. I hope you're right, though I wish this effort wasn't required. Our dynamic was lovely before. I don't want to have to adjust for a grouch." I start to get up. "I don't want to waste my evening. I think I'll work on my artwork for a bit. Do you want to watch our show later?"

"You bet, sounds good. Enjoy." He surprises me by walking over and pulling me into a firm hug. It has been a long time since we've had physical contact, and we've never been very touchy-feely friends. It feels amazing. My hands rest lightly on the muscles of his back. I feel comforted, smelling his familiar scent, even though I'm far from at peace regarding all of this. He releases me too quickly, smiles without meeting my eyes, and leaves my room.

I sigh. He's just being kind. I turn to my artwork and pull out my paints. My heart feels a little lighter.

Chapter 7

I'm having trouble sleeping despite my efforts to have a relaxing evening before going to bed. The day must have affected me more than I thought. It feels like I've been awake for hours, but I know I've been sleeping off and on because I have vague memories of dreams. Thank goodness it's Saturday and I can sleep in, if I can ever get myself to sleep.

I roll over again and hug my teddy bear against my chest. Inhaling through my nose and exhaling through my mouth, I deliberately relax my face and body and try to clear my mind. Maybe I can finally rest.

I'm in a grassy park staring at a familiar skyline. Where have I seen this place before? The colorful and eclectic city glows in the sunset's light. I'm uneasy, but I don't know why. I want something. An idea pops into my mind. I look over my shoulder and see a man leaning in the shade of a nearby tree. He's examining his fingernails intently, but I get the impression he was just watching me.

I walk over to him and say, "Hey. Do you know where I could get… a treat?"

His head snaps up, and he looks up at me with eyes that seem to naturally crinkle at the corners, even if he isn't smiling with his mouth. Up close, he looks familiar.

"I sure do!" He looks pleased.

I hold my hand out to him. Taking it, he pulls me in the direction of a disreputable-looking bar.

"Wait. Is this place pink-and-white striped or green and gold inside?" I ask.

Before pushing the door open, he pauses and turns to face me, giving me his full attention.

"Pink and white *or* green and gold?" His tone is teasing. His face becomes serious when he sees I'm not kidding. "I'm not sure, it's possible. Is everything all right? Do you want to go somewhere else?"

I mentally shake myself and smile up at him. "No, I'm fine. This place is fine." I nod in what I hope appears a convincing manner.

He doesn't look convinced.

"You're always saying that you're 'fine.' Makes me think

you aren't so fine." Not waiting for a response, he opens the door and ushers me inside.

I breathe a sigh of relief when I see the turquoise plastic tabletops and sparkly red vinyl benches of the diner. A waitress in torn jeans and an '80s band shirt takes my order.

Once she's gone, I look back at my companion. He's still familiar. We've met before, I'm sure of it, but I can't quite place him. He's staring at me in an expectant way but doesn't say anything. I suspect he knows something but wants me to work it out for myself. He fiddles with the tabletop jukebox.

Here goes. "Sorry, I'm having trouble figuring out what's happening. I think I've been here before, but at the same time, I don't think I have." I fiddle with my utensils. "And I think I know you."

He looks up and nods encouragingly. "We've met, but only briefly, and you were here before. Twice."

Munching on a piece of fried zucchini, I try to understand. All the questions in my head vie to be the next one I ask.

"Can you explain what's going on? Who are you? What is this place?" I finally ask.

"You're here. I'm Adrian Vagary, and this is Scape W2PF1L."

Talk about unhelpful. "What the heck does 'Scape W2PF1L' mean?"

Again, he gives me an odd look. "I'm not sure what else you want me to say. I don't have more explanation for you than that. This is W2PF1L. I've been here... awhile. Before here I was at AA8M, and before that it was B4MW2, and I think before that it was—"

"Never mind that!" I cut him off. "What do you do here?"

"This is where I work."

If looks could kill…

He looks at me blandly in return. "Sorry. Clearly, I'm not answering your questions well enough. Let's go to the Ferris wheel." Awkwardly, he waves in the direction of the carnival. It's like he expects me to lead the way.

"What?" But he doesn't respond and instead grabs my hand and yanks me out onto the street.

I find myself blindly following him through the most winding and wonderous city I've ever seen.

Sidewalk vendors hock cantaloupes, balloon animals, scrolls, and skateboards. Colorful skyscrapers abut black-and-white barbershops and log cabins. The cobblestones beneath my feet are sometimes asphalt with yellow stripes down the middle, and at other times dusty dirt or red brick. I know Adrian is in front of me holding my hand, but I'm absorbed with all the visual stimuli surrounding me. I forget to talk. Minutes or maybe hours later, we stop.

"We're here!" he gleefully announces, waving his free arm out in an expansive movement. "It's looking particularly beautiful today."

I gaze at the most glorious vista I've ever seen. We're at the top of a rolling mountain range, and the view in front of us must stretch for hundreds of miles. Instead of trees and wilderness, everything before me is candy. The sun is setting and everything is bathed in gold. Translucent gumdrop meadows catch the light, sending shimmering rainbow effects along the ground. Sugar-crested mountaintops sparkle in the gilded light. Spiral lollypop forests cascade down hills and fade into the distance. It's breathtaking.

"C'mon, let's take a ride," he says.

I turn and see the ticketing line for an enormous Ferris wheel. I smile at him and let him pull me into a red gondola when the beep from my alarm jolts me back into my bedroom. The last thing I see in my mind's eye is his disappointed face.

I knock on Jeremy's cracked open door and peek in. He's on his computer playing a video game, but when he sees me, he pauses and lowers his headset to his neck. "Hey, what's up?" he asks.

"Can I talk to you a minute?" We've been doing better lately, but I'm still nervous he might resist more personal encounters.

He sets his headset on his desk, swivels his computer chair to face me, and gestures to the straight wooden chair that sits next to his desk, where Bob's currently curled up. I pick up Bob to loud protests and sit down. Bob spends a few moments deciding if he's offended enough to jump down, decides he's not, and curls back up on my lap. I give him a couple strokes before bringing my attention back to Jeremy. He waits patiently for me to start talking.

"Sorry, I feel kind of weird about this," I say.

He looks alarmed for a second.

"I'm having recurring dreams."

Jeremy relaxes visibly. "So these are different than the hypnagogic hallucinations?" he asks.

"Yeah, those have always just blurred the lines at the cusp between sleep and awake. These ones aren't like that. They're recurring, but not in the way I've experienced occasionally, where I can continue a dream if I focus on it as I'm falling asleep. These feel real, and the story seems to continue from where the prior one left off. Sorta."

"Are they scary?"

"No, not at all. At worst, they're sometimes a little unsettling." I pause for a moment, considering if I should tell him everything. I've had abnormal dreams since I was a kid. I think they started before I met Jeremy. We've talked about them almost from the beginning of our friendship. I started seeing sleep specialists soon after meeting Jeremy, and he was always interested and supportive. He has always been nonjudgmental about my dreams. Even so, it's still hard to admit my mind does strange things sometimes. "I think what's bothering me about them is that I met a man in one a few days ago and he keeps showing up too. And what's even weirder is that he remembers me from past times I've been there. I know it's a dream and in my head, but it feels real, like I'm getting to know him."

I wonder if I imagine Jeremy's eyes dimming a bit, but I know he's listening and considering what I've told him. He doesn't have sympathetic experience to help with this situation, as he mostly doesn't recall his dreams. When he does, they fall well within the realm of normal.

He adjusts his shoulders. "Why is it bad to get to know him?" he inquires after a minute.

"He's not real, Jeremy, he's in my head."

"So? He's not having you do unsafe things or directing your thoughts to bad places, is he?"

I shake my head.

"He's a recurring character. I'm no sleep expert, but it doesn't sound bad to me. As you said, kinda weird. But if it's bothering you, maybe you should make another appointment with your sleep doctor, to follow up and see what she thinks."

Now why didn't I think of that? Over the years, I've gotten used to my strange dream experiences, and I haven't needed regular appointments with sleep specialists, but I do occasionally have an unnerving experience and want a second opinion. I think it's normal to find sleep hallucinations disconcerting, since they bridge the barrier that is normally firmly defined between sleep and awake. A couple years ago, I went down the rabbit hole of distrusting what actions I might do in that middle time where I'm neither fully awake nor fully asleep. Dr. Gallegos soothed my worries with her understanding, expertise, and practical view of my sleep experiences. She assuaged my fear that I might act in a way that could be concerning or harmful.

"That's such a good idea, Jeremy," I say, feeling lighter than I have in a while, smiling into his eyes. "On Monday, I'll schedule an appointment with her." I stand up to leave, cradling Bob in my arms.

"You could also start keeping a dream journal again the way you did when we were kids. What's his name?"

"Who?" My mind's still on the journal idea.

He looks at me in disbelief. "The guy, Val. The dream guy."

"Oh!" I laugh. "It's Adrian."

"Psh, Adrian." He winks at me. "Sounds like someone who *would* be haunting your dreams."

I pretend to be offended. "He's not *haunting* my dreams, Jere, he's just a character. He's nice, actually." Again the guarded look comes to Jeremy's eyes. I knew I didn't imagine it earlier. I wonder if he's jealous.

"Just don't go falling in love with someone imaginary." The words are light, but his tone comes out serious. He clears his throat. "Then you'd have to get more help than just a sleep doctor." He waggles his eyebrows, his tone joking now.

"I would never fall in love with someone imaginary," I scoff, as I turn to leave the room. "Thanks for listening. I appreciate your insight." I glance over my shoulder, and he briefly meets my eyes and nods before turning back to his computer, putting his headset back on.

Chapter 8

VALANCY

"Folks are going to think you're coming back just to see me," an amused voice says behind me.

I whirl around, taking in the green parkland around me, before my eyes settle on the source of the voice.

"You! I know you!"

Mock innocently, he asks, "Do you? Where do you know me from?"

I roll my eyes. "From here, of course. Your name is…" I struggle to recall. "…Darrian?"

"Adrian," he corrects. He looks surprised and perhaps pleased. Hesitantly, he asks, "Do you want to get a snack?"

I look at him askance, crossing my arms and popping my hip. "Is that always how you start conversations? We've already had a snack together multiple times. What I'd love to do is ride the Ferris wheel. I missed out on that last time. C'mon!" I grab his hand, and his face registers actual shock. Laughing, I drag him in the direction of the fair.

I'm not sure how I know my way through the mismatched city but before I know it, we're standing in front of the wheel, and Adrian is getting tickets. He still has a slightly stunned look as he holds his hand out to help me into a yellow gondola.

Taking a seat across from me, he looks at me apprehensively. "A-are you afraid of heights?" he stammers.

"No, are you?"

"No…. That's kind of unusual. Most people only ride this if they're afraid of heights."

"Are they trying to get over their fear?"

He looks confused and shakes his head firmly. "No, I don't think that's the motivation."

"Seems weird to subject yourself to something you're afraid of if there's no intention to try and overcome it."

He seems genuinely perplexed. "Huh, I never thought about it that way."

I look out at the view. Confection conifers coated in sugar crystals line the Jell-O mold mountains that stretch off into the distance. It's sunset again. Why is it always sunset? I shake my head to clear obtrusive thoughts I don't have the answers to. I turn back to Adrian.

"Why do you bring people here if you know they'll be afraid of it?" I ask.

He seems confused. "I don't make them come here."

"But you suggest it."

"Yes, but they can say no. They just don't."

"So do you enjoy riding rides with people who are terrified?"

"It's my job," he says matter-of-factly.

"Your job? Whose job is it to join people on adventures they don't enjoy?"

"Mine."

"Never mind, this isn't going anywhere."

"Obviously. The Ferris wheel only goes in circles. Although one time…" He drifts off when he sees my expression. "Sorry? Is that not what you meant?"

I look away from him and see a toaster with a pattern of buttercups painted on its side fly by with a mouse as its pilot. I blink and refocus on Adrian. How can he be this obtuse? This whole place is bewildering, and his responses to my questions don't lessen my confusion.

"What is this place?"

"I told you last time, this is Scape W2PF1L."

"Reciting random strings of characters doesn't explain what scapes are or why I keep coming here. I haven't always come here, and I don't think this is where I always am." I pause as I try to figure out what I'm trying to say. I can't wrap my head around the void that surrounds my thoughts in this place. I feel like I don't only exist here, but I can't recall what the rest of my life is like. A mental veil blocks it from view. I give up and proceed with my interrogation. "And why does it seem to start over from the same point every time?"

He considers my questions. The breeze ruffles his hair, causing some hairs to stand out from his head.

He shakes his head. "I don't know why this is happening with you; it's new for me too. The scapes are set up to provide basic environments for visitors, which can be altered as needed by the visitor's preferences. I will say that typically guests visit a scape, move about it in the predictable way, albeit with their personal adjustments, and then leave. Occasionally, someone will bounce between scapes a bit and their visits generally seem more erratic while they're visiting, but I don't know specifically why that happens. This situation with you is a new one for me. I've never had someone come back. Or if they have, it's been long enough in between that it's not memorable for me or them. I've never recognized anyone."

"Has anyone ever recognized you?" I ask.

"That's harder to answer because, by nature, my appearance alters as the scape's does to their personal preferences. So… yes… sometimes they do seem to know me based on my appearance, but not from attributes associated with the real me or because of prior interactions with me. Does that make sense?"

It doesn't, but I believe him. I move on to something else he mentioned. "When you say, 'they leave,' what do you mean by that?"

"Like last time you were here, we were going to get on the ride, but then you disappeared."

"I see." I don't see at all. "What happens to you after someone leaves?"

"I'm still here."

"But what do you do?"

"Whatever I want. I go to the bar and have something to eat, hang out at my apartment. You know, normal stuff. I do whatever I want until it's time to go meet a new visitor."

"Do you always meet them in the park?"

"No, sometimes I meet them at the top of the Ferris wheel, or in a café, or at a random place where I can give them directions to the bathroom."

"I haven't seen any bathrooms."

"There aren't any."

"Then how do you give them directions?"

"Just because there aren't any bathrooms doesn't mean I can't give them directions. They want directions. I provide that."

"I would think it would be more helpful to get them to a bathroom if that's what they want."

He shudders. "As someone who has been to bathrooms in other scapes, you do not want to go to one of the bathrooms. They're the foulest part of the scapes. They're filthy and overflowing, with no doors or privacy. It's a horrible experience. Trust me, the bathrooms are the worst."

I make a face. I've only imagined bathrooms that foul. "That does sound awful. Still, it seems strange to provide directions to nowhere instead of trying to help them."

He looks at me oddly. "But that's my job. I'm here to provide what visitors want."

"But what they want is a bathroom."

"No, they most certainly do *not* want a bathroom. What they want is directions, and that's what I provide." He smiles guilelessly at me.

I give up. Clearly, I don't understand.

"So, what are you providing for me?" I ask, changing tactics.

He looks uncertain. "Well, you said you wanted to ride the wheel. Here we are."

"You don't seem very confident in that answer."

Now he looks frustrated. "I'm not." His words are agitated. "This whole situation is disconcerting for me. You're much more aware of me than most visitors are, and now this is the fourth time we've met. I don't have a precedent for this situation, and I'm not sure what I'm supposed to do. Typically, I'm just here for the ride, so to speak, and a sounding board for the visitor's desires. But you look at *me*, the real me, and you ask questions about me as an individual, not some fantasy you've projected onto me. Even the first time we met, you looked at me several times, and I never felt myself become anything other than how I am."

This is a lot to digest. "How does your appearance change with others?"

"Visitors alter my appearance to match their ideas. The same way the food, décor, and waitress are different every time we go to that bar. I can be whoever you want me to be."

"But this"—I motion up and down in his direction—"is how you look when you get ready in the morning, before anyone has influenced you?"

He inspects himself. He's wearing a brown bomber jacket, a worn green T-shirt, and jeans. He nods. "Yes, this is how I looked at home before coming to work. When I play a less active role in a visit or when my appearance doesn't have significance, this is how I appear, and also how I look again after guests leave and everything reverts."

I consider this. Most of what he's telling me makes no sense, but underneath all the chaos I hear sincerity. This man isn't lying to me; he believes what he's telling me. What's more unsettling is that he finds this situation as weird as I do. In a world where Adrian goes with the flow of others, I'm different.

We're at the top, stopped to let passengers on. The wind is blowing strongly, whipping my hair around my face. The views are stunning. I take a deep breath and absorb it all, feeling a moment of peace in this whirlwind of information. Despite how implausible this all seems, I like Adrian. He seems to be honest, kind, and guileless. I look over at him and smile. He smiles back, and his whole face lights up.

I wake up.

I slept in more than I typically do for a weekend, which is refreshing since I haven't been resting well lately. Having another disconcerting dream about Adrian isn't my favorite, but getting a good night's sleep will make today more pleasant. There's nothing I hate more than when my weekend gets trashed due to poor sleep. It adds insult to injury.

Jeremy is going hiking with some friends today. He was out of the house before I woke up. I take my time getting myself together, enjoying a leisurely bath instead of my typical shower and scrambling eggs to go with my toast and tea. It's nice to have the morning to myself. I also dig out my old, partially filled journal and record details from this latest Adrian dream. I try to add a few tidbits I can recall from earlier dreams with him before placing it alongside a pen on my bedside table.

After starting laundry, I pick up my cell phone to call my dad. He lives in Taos, New Mexico now, and I don't see him as often. I try to catch up with him regularly by phone.

He picks up the phone after two rings. "Hey, Valley, how's my girl?"

"Hi, Daddy. I'm good. How are you and Marge doing?" Margorie is my stepmom whom my dad married eight years ago. After my mom died when I was twenty, it took him a few years to recover, and he met Marge in a surviving spouses' grief support group they were both attending. She has been awesome for him, and it eased my worries that he found someone to have a second chance with. We still talk about Mom sometimes, but I'm glad he has been able to move on with his life. I think Mom would be glad too.

"Oh, you know, honey, we're old."

I feel a stab of alarm and say with trepidation, "What does *that* mean?"

He bursts out a full belly laugh. "I'm sorry, sweetie, I forget how you stress about things. Marge is fine. We *are* old, but none of our complaints are any more serious than feeling a little stiff and having to be on some maintenance prescriptions."

I exhale a sigh of relief.

"I promise, if there ever is anything more serious, I won't hide it from you or be cryptic about it. You have my word."

I laugh ruefully. "Thank you, Dad. I appreciate that more than you know."

"Of course. Sorry for scaring you. Now, moving on, tell me about work."

"Oh… work is fine," I hedge.

He chuckles. "You're just like your mom, can't hide your feelings well. Is it going that badly?"

Calling my dad was a mistake. Not really, but he always sees through me. It would be nice to have some illusion of mystery. "I wouldn't say that things are going badly, exactly. There's a new guy who has thrown a monkey wrench in our work dynamic."

"Ah, I see. That can be hard to handle. Want to tell me about it?"

My dad stays on the phone for forty-five minutes, listening to me vent about Clarance. Talking to him and getting his advice helps me feel less worried about the long-term effects of Clarance being part of our team. My dad has had many jobs over the years and has his fair share of crazy coworker stories to share and learn from.

I don't tell him about my dreams with Adrian. For a down-to-earth guy like my dad, that topic seems out of his element. When I was dealing with dream issues as a kid, he mostly deferred to Mom because he couldn't wrap his head around it. Also, he would be more likely to worry about that than an ornery coworker situation.

When Jeremy gets back from his outdoor adventure, I'm stirring chili on the stove.

"That smells delicious. I'm starving." Dropping his pack on the floor where he might remember to pick it up when he leaves the kitchen, he comes over behind me and tries to peek in the pot.

"Ahhh! You're all sweaty and gross!" I leap out of the way and defend the chili with a wooden spoon. "Go take a shower. This still needs about half an hour to simmer before it's ready."

He throws up his hands in defeat. "Fine, fine, I'll go get cleaned up. Better to wash off the glorious outdoors than sample chili that isn't ready yet."

I brandish the spoon menacingly so he doesn't change his mind. I hear his laughter from down the hall.

Chapter 9

VALANCY

This time when I enter the scape, I'm in the candy hills on the other side of the Ferris wheel, seeing the sunset-illuminated city from a distance. It's stunning. The buildings glow in every color imaginable. Purple brick buildings with green-and-azure striped awnings sparkle next to shimmering powder blue skyscrapers.

I tear my eyes away and inspect my surroundings. It's beautiful here too, different up close. I'm standing on a green sugar hill with patches of peppermint night-blooming cereus flowers swaying in the breeze. The dirt beneath the grass might be cocoa powder; I stoop and reach out my hand to check.

I hear running footsteps approaching. I stand back up, licking my fingers—definitely chocolate—as Adrian crests the hill, out of breath.

"Why'd you show up here? No one ever shows up here."

He must be joking. "You know I have zero control over this situation, right?"

"That's not true! You have. Loads of control. The details. Are all you," he puffs out between breaths.

"So you say, but it's not something I'm actively aware of doing."

He looks exasperated. "Just because you aren't consciously trying, it doesn't mean you can't. If you don't like it, you can change it."

"I'm quite happy being on this hill; it's you who seems annoyed by it." I smile smugly at him.

He looks unamused, his chest still heaving.

"Fine." I concede that I'm curious. "If I wanted to have a more active role in changing things, how would I do that?"

Still breathing hard, he holds up a finger. "Give me a moment."

After he wheezes back to normal breathing, Adrian straightens and smiles. His annoyance and discomfiture vanish, and he runs his fingers distractingly through his hair to tidy it.

"Okay, let's practice. What's something you want?" he asks.

"Something I want?"

"Yes! Anything." He smiles expectantly.

Initially, I think of a cup of tea or a swimming pool, but I'm feeling exasperated with him and this confusing world, and I want to indulge my pettiness for a moment. "My request is an enraged bull with dilated nostrils emanating steam."

His expression of horror is comical. It makes me laugh.

"Fine, fine, I'll think of something else." I wave my hand in an appeasing way.

He doesn't look happy. "I'm not sure that can be undone so easily."

"I mean, do you see a raging bull running around?" I gesture to the beautiful, calm slopes surrounding us.

"Shhh!" he cautions, waving his hands to suppress me. "Stop mentioning it," he hisses.

"You don't want a livid purple bull to come charging over this peaceful hill?" I ask innocently.

He's really on edge now. "Please, Valancy, I implore you. I'm not kidding about your ability to influence this place. Suggestions like that can manifest."

"Maybe you should counter-manifest." My response is feisty.

"I can't. Only you and other guests can." He looks around nervously. A buttered toast fly bumps into him and Adrian yelps and jumps.

I sigh, yielding that I'm being more unkind to him than I'd intended. "I'm sorry, I'll stop teasing you. What I actually want is a tea set. Oh! Make that a china tea set! That way when the bull shows up, he can charge through it and I can say, 'A bull in a china shop!'" I couldn't help myself. I grasp my stomach, laughing loudly. My eyes water. When I've finally gotten control of myself, I look at Adrian.

He's standing there, looking annoyed and puzzled.

"What?" I ask.

"Why would a bull charge through a china shop? That's a terrible location. Wouldn't everything break?"

I'm at a loss. "Have you never heard that expression before?"

"No, I can't say I have," he says drily.

"It's an idiom. A bull in a china shop wouldn't be careful around the delicate objects and would probably make a huge mess of everything. You'd say that if someone barged into a situation or didn't take care of someone else's feelings."

"I see." I don't think he does. "Anyway," he moves on, "so a china tea set is what you want?" He looks less enthusiastic than he did originally, and I feel a tinge of regret for causing him stress. I allow myself to be led back to the original conversation.

"Yes."

"Tell me about this tea set." He hear him sigh with what I assume is relief that I'm going along with this discussion and not continuing to pursue the bull idea. He has been nothing but kind to me; I can do better.

"It's porcelain and extremely delicate. The cups are a little too wide and tend to slosh if filled too full."

He nods encouragingly. "What's the design?"

I picture them in my mind. "They're an off-white eggshell with pink roses and green leaves. Gold rims and accents."

"What pieces are included in this set?"

"Two cups, two saucers, cream pot, sugar bowl with tongs

for the sugar cubes, and teapot brimming with hot tea. All on a lacquered wooden tray that has painted handles to match."

"What will you do with this tea set once you have it?"

"I'll sit here on the grass with you, and we'll have a tea party." I smile at him.

He smiles back. "Where should we sit?" he asks.

"It doesn't matter, since this mythical tea service doesn't exist."

He gestures to my hands. I look down at the tea set I just described. All the details are there as I said them; even more so, how I saw them in my mind's eye. Plus, there is a matching serving plate with tiny green and pink macarons.

I gasp. Then I glance at him. He has a pink-and-white checkered picnic blanket over one arm, and two green cushions under the other. "But I didn't ask for these additional items!"

"Doesn't matter. They showed up because you subconsciously thought of them or associated them with the tea set or this location. See how everything matches?"

I nod, looking back at my tray. Steam is seeping from the teapot's spout. I try to wrap my head around what just happened. I knew this place shifted, but this immediate and deliberate change is simultaneously unnerving and magical.

"C'mon, Valancy, let's find a good place to have your tea party." Adrian beams at me and starts heading farther along the ridge toward an open space.

I exhale and tear my eyes away from the tea tray. This

place confuses me, but turning down a beautiful tea party is unfathomable. I need to accept and enjoy this moment as it has been given to me.

Adrian laughs, seeing my consternation and loving it.

I follow him to a nice spot where he spreads the blanket out. He sits on one side, and I kneel on the other and place the tray carefully between us.

"You pour," he says.

I grin broadly and pick up the teapot. Some dreams do come true. "How do you take your tea?" I ask regally, lifting a delicate cup and saucer in my other hand.

With a serious expression, he responds, "Two lumps of sugar and the barest hint of cream."

I nod. "Of course. A proper way to take one's tea."

We giggle companionably as we enjoy our tea picnic. He exaggeratedly sticks out his pinky, even though his hands are too big to use the handle properly and the tea sloshes over the sides a bit. We oooh and aaah over the macarons. The interminable sunset continues its nonexistent descent, bathing the landscape in golden light. This is perfection.

I'm enjoying the view and feeling completely content and full, when a snorting, raging, violet-colored bull with a gold ring in its nose charges over the hill. Adrian and I yelp and dive in opposite directions as the bull tramples through the middle of our dishes.

I sit up in bed with a gasp. "Run from the bull!" I yelp. My room is silent except for the faint swishing of the overhead fan. My heartrate slows as reality comes back into focus.

I reach for my dream journal and write down a few details by the light of my cell phone before lying back with a sigh and closing my eyes again. I manage to doze until my alarm goes off.

Chapter 10
VALANCY

Before work, I log in to my patient portal for Doctor Gallegos's office and make a tele-health appointment for tomorrow afternoon. It's before the end of the workday, but Mark always encourages us to take personal time off as needed. I can leave work early and come home for my appointment. After submitting the online forms, I breathe a sigh of relief. Taking steps in a positive direction always makes me feel better.

The drive to work feels less tense than it has lately, although the undertone of dread regarding Clarance is still making itself felt. I give myself a pep talk about the importance of workplace harmony and trying to find ways to connect with Clarance. I almost successfully ignore the voice in my head, which sounds suspiciously like Daphne, telling me he doesn't deserve my efforts. Whether he does or not, I care about workplace peace and I'm going to keep trying. Not forever, that would be masochistic, but for now.

The stars are aligned in my favor today; Clarence's car isn't there when I pull in. I unlock The Paint Palette and breathe in its familiar scents: scented candles from a display, dried paint, window cleaner, and a tiny hint of dust. I take my time walking around, flipping on the lights. It feels like it has been too long since I've been here alone. The Palette has been my home away from home for five years, but for the past week it hasn't been the same. I walk around and look at some of the updated displays someone else, maybe Daphne, set up. I run my fingers lightly over some new textile pieces. As I reconnect with the gallery, my heart lightens.

The bells on the door chime and I tense until I see it's Mark bustling in with Daphne jogging up behind him, catching the door before it closes.

"Good morning!" Mark waves as he heads in the direction of his office.

Daphne detours in my direction. "Checking out my new displays?" She motions to the textiles.

"I was! They're gorgeous."

She smiles, pleased at the praise. We browse around together. Neither of us mentions Clarance, but I'm sure we're both thinking how nice it is that he isn't here. This is how it used to feel before he came. I miss this.

After a couple minutes, Mark comes back out into the Main Gallery. "Hey, I got a voicemail from Clarance. His daughter isn't feeling well, so she couldn't go to school today. He's home until the sitter can go over to stay with her."

"Oh," I say, caught off guard. "I didn't know he had a daughter."

"Yeah, he showed me a picture. I think she's around eight or nine."

I'm still a bit stunned. Clarance being a dad doesn't mesh well into the grumpy hermit story I've built for him in my head.

"Is Clarance married?" Daphne asks. My head snaps in her direction and then to Mark as I'm suddenly desperately curious about Clarance's relationship status.

"He's never mentioned a spouse. I've always gotten the impression he's a single dad." Clearly, Mark has had more meaningful interactions with Clarance than I have. This realization annoys me because I've been trying to connect with him and have apparently entirely failed. I didn't have an inkling about some of the most important elements of his life. In fact, I don't know anything personal about him at all.

I only have a few minutes to dwell on this before the day picks up pace and I'm distracted by tasks at hand.

Clarance eventually appears around lunchtime, which works out perfectly for me to avoid him for an hour while I eat. Although I'm not sure I actively needed to avoid him today, as he's noticeably distracted and withdrawn the few times we cross paths. He keeps to himself, working on his own projects, and mercifully not interfering with mine. He's the first out the door when we close.

I wave goodbye to Daphne and then to Mark as he's locking the door. I breathe a sigh of contentment as I walk to my car. Today was an unexpectedly good day.

***

I pull out a red velvet cake mix. Jeremy texted that he's working late this evening, and I feel like baking while I have the house to myself. I'm in a good mood. I enjoy baking, but I have to be in the mood for it. I hum as I mix ingredients.

The fragrance from the oven has started to permeate the kitchen when Jeremy comes in. I'm sitting at the table reading, and I hear him go to his room and move around on his side of the house. A few minutes pass, and he comes into the kitchen and drops his lunchbox on the counter next to the sink.

"Baking muffins?"

"A cake." I look up from my book. He's peering in the oven's window.

"Even better. Today was a good day?" He knows my baking habits.

"It was! I got an appointment with Dr. Gallegos for tomorrow, and Clarance didn't show up till noon cuz his daughter has a cold."

"He has a daughter?" Jeremy asks incredulously.

"I know! That surprised me too. But it was nice to have a break from him and reconnect with Daphne and Mark."

"I'm glad you had a nicer day."

"Me too. How was your day?"

He sits in his chair across from me and slouches down, getting comfortable. "It was long, but good, I suppose. Just dealing with some deadlines, but everything is on track. It's a lot of work, but not a lot of stress." He leans back and rolls his neck side to side. When he straightens again, he asks, "Have you had more Adrian dreams?" He sounds uncomfortable.

There is no point in lying for his comfort. "I have. I took your advice and started keeping a dream journal again."

He nods and looks away from me out the window.

"Do these dreams upset you?" I ask. "You've been kinda weird about them."

He shakes his head and turns back to me, a smile pasted on his face. "No, of course not."

"You sure?" Sometimes Jeremy needs a little prodding to open up.

"Positive." He nods firmly. "Weird dreams and Valancy are synonymous in my mind. I'm sure there's no cause for alarm."

"What about the subject of my dreams?" I press.

His face falls and he looks away. Maybe my suspicion that he's jealous of Adrian isn't misplaced.

"No, don't be silly, it would be stupid to be upset by what your subconscious comes up with."

"Jeremy, you're allowed to have feelings about this, even if they seem illogical."

"Am I?" He sounds wistful, still gazing out the window. Suddenly, he turns to look at me and the expression in his eyes makes my heart stutter. I can't look away. The moment draws out, and I don't know what to say. Finally, I open my mouth to say... anything... and the timer on the oven dings.

I leap out of my seat and scramble to remove the cake and stick a toothpick in the center. I keep busy as long as possible, giving myself time to regain my composure. When I finally turn back to the table, Jeremy's gone. I breathe a sigh of relief. Whatever just happened, it's over for now.

I don't see him for the rest of the evening. His door is closed, and he doesn't come and check on the status of the cake. After I frost it and cut myself a piece, I take it to my room and text him that the cake is ready. He responds with an unsatisfying thumbs up. I hear noise from the kitchen, but he never comes by my room to thank me. He does send a brief text: *It's delicious, thanks.*

"You vanished at the perfect time to avoid all the mess." Adrian's voice is peeved.

"I thought you said things revert after I leave. Didn't the mess just vanish?"

I lean back on my swing to ease myself higher and raise my face to the sky and wind as I smirk. I glance down at him; he's sitting on a swing stubbing the toe of his shoe into the dirt. His whole body is a grumble. I cover my mouth to avoid laughing out loud again, which causes my swing to veer. I regain control of myself and the swing. "I'm sorry, Adrian. I know it was all my fault. I shouldn't have mentioned the bu—"

"Don't!" He looks up at me and raises his hand, as though to ward off a blow.

"What did I do?"

"We do not need that *thing* to be manifested again." He looks at me seriously until first his eyes crinkle and then his mouth devolves into laughter. I join him, and we share a long belly laugh. When his chuckles finally die down, he starts to swing, pumping his legs to gain height and speed.

Finally, we ease up and bring our swings to a stop. We're silent. I'm enjoying the view of the city.

"This is a beautiful place," I say. I glance over at him.

He nods, gazing at the skyline. "It sure is. It's the most beautiful I've ever seen it."

"Sunset is a beautiful time of day."

"Yes. Yes, that must be it."

Chapter 11

VALANCY

I glance at the front desk as I walk in the door of The Palette. Clarance looks up and smiles, which I still find unsettling, particularly now that it's directed at me. His face seems surprised when he decides to use it for a smile.

"Good morning, Valancy."

"Hi, Clarance?" I respond, feeling ill at ease. I hate hearing the question mark at the end, but this is unexpectedly normal for him and it's making me feel on edge. *Who are you and what have you done with my grumpy coworker?*

"You're leaving early today?"

"Yes, I am. There shouldn't be any issue with coverage." I hate the defensiveness I hear in my voice.

"I'm sure it'll work out fine; just wanted to make sure I knew the plan." He goes back to studying the papers on the desk, still looking remarkably calm and peaceful. He wipes his nose on a tissue and takes a sip of water before he looks up again. He seems surprised I'm still there. "Can I help you with something?"

"Oh. Yes. Sorry." I get a hold of myself, smiling quickly to cover my discomfort. "I wanted to tell you I was sorry to hear your daughter was sick."

He smiles slightly again; this is really throwing me for a loop. "Thanks. She's feeling better today. It was only a cold."

"Good to hear. Getting sick is more stressful since the pandemic."

He nods in agreement. Apparently, that's one thing we agree about.

I head for my desk.

Clarance and I don't interact much for the rest of the day, but the feeling at work is noticeably less strained than it has been. When I leave at 2:00 to head home for my appointment, Clarance wishes me a good rest of my day. I feel bad for doubting his intentions, but the change is so sudden I'm finding it difficult to not be suspicious.

***

"Hello, Ms. Strickland, it's nice to see you again."

"Yeah, you too, Dr. G! I'm glad you had an opening the same week I looked."

"I love tele-health for that reason. They're easy to fit in

shorter windows, especially for established patients. Want to tell me what's going on?" Dr. Gallegos is middle-aged and slender. She wears her long, dark hair that has a few silvery strands in a braid over her shoulder. With her white lab coat, she presents a comfortingly knowledgeable appearance on my laptop screen.

"We've talked about my hypnagogic hallucinations before."

She looks at her notes. "And the hypnopompic."

"Yes." I've never been able to tell if my vivid dreams happen as I'm falling asleep or as I'm waking up. I always call them hypnogogic because it rolls off the tongue better. Hypnopompic always reminds me of "pompous" or something.

"Has something changed with them?"

"Yes, I'm having recurring dreams. Not the hallucinations, but still unusual. More accurately, I have a specific dream that keeps happening over and over."

"Tell me about it." She looks at me with interest through the screen. Her body's relaxed, and she appears ready to hear what I have to say.

"I always go to this same place. It changes slightly from dream to dream, but the main setting is consistent, and there's always a man there. The dreams follow each other in a uniform time, picking up where the prior one left off. It's not an identical dream over and over; it's a continuation, but in the same environment."

"Is it alarming? Does it frighten you? Do you know the man?"

"Only when I wake up do I feel unsettled by it because I see the connection to prior dreams, but while I'm there it's pleasant enough. It feels like a place I'm visiting. The man is nice, and we have interesting conversations. I think we're becoming friends. He isn't someone I recognize from the real world, though."

"Why does it bother you after you wake up?"

"Because Adrian—that's his name—says he lives in this dream world, and he sees, I suppose, dreamers, all the time, but he also finds it surprising that he keeps seeing me again and again. When I wake up and can view everything with clarity, it feels weird."

"I see. It does sound unsettling." She pauses for a moment, looking elsewhere on her screen. After she has collected her thoughts, she continues. "Sleep hallucinations are a strange phenomenon, but they aren't dangerous. They're not an indicator of mental illness or correlated to concerning conditions. They can be distressing, certainly, but I don't think you need to worry about your mental health."

I already knew that.

She continues. "As with many things regarding sleep, there is still much we don't know, but this situation doesn't sound dangerous. As we've discussed in the past, your hallucinations seem to be exacerbated by stress, and that may also affect how vivid your dreams are. Have you been particularly stressed lately?"

I nod. "Yes, there have been various things going on at work and in my personal life recently that've been stressing me out. These dreams are starting to add to that."

"That's understandable. Vivid dreams are a common and normal sleep occurrence that happens to everyone. While recurring dreams are less common, they're still well within normal expectations and can be triggered by stress. What's more unusual about your recurring dream is that it's not a nightmare. Most recurring dreams are negative. You have that to be grateful for!" She smiles.

I guess I should be glad that Adrian and I aren't fighting zombies every night.

"All that being said, if these dreams continue, I think we should probably plan to test you for sleep apnea, in case you have something additional going on. It's certainly not urgent, more to rule it out as a possibility. Reach out to my office in a month or so if the dreams haven't resolved on their own, and we'll get that process moving along."

"That sounds like a good plan to me," I agree. I'm glad she has a game plan.

"Okay, great." She moves along briskly. "In the meantime, I have a few things I want us to focus on to help you with this while these dreams are part of your sleep. To start, try not to worry too much about them. I know that's easier said than done, but they don't sound concerning, and from what you've said, they're pleasant while you're experiencing them. Unless they get noticeably more alarming, let them happen as long as they're going to. They'll likely pass eventually, when your stressful situations change or resolve."

I make an unconvinced face, and she chuckles. "You're allowed to be stressed and work it out over time. Quick fixes don't really exist in the realm of sleep conditions. You're always welcome to call me if you want to check if something sounds concerning. I'm sure work is contributing to your stress, but that doesn't mean that will last forever, or that you won't find ways to adapt and cope. Stressors are often worse when they're new. What we want to see is improvement, such as these dreams occurring less frequently."

That makes sense.

"To segue from that, the next thing I want you to focus on are ways you can manage the stress in your life and other things we can do to make sure everything is all right and back to normal soon. You've always known that stress is a contributing factor for your disturbed sleep. Maybe we can figure out some behaviors and techniques to help you manage that and get you back to normal sleep patterns more quickly."

***

Jeremy is back to being distant with me. When he came home today, he immediately went to his room and closed the door. I miss the lighthearted interactions we'd slowly been coming back to lately. Why do feelings have to spoil things? This is the "personal life" stress I mentioned to Dr. G, in case that wasn't obvious.

I'm stirring noodles for pasta when he comes in later. He sits on the sofa in the den. He's close enough to talk to, but far enough away to limit conversation. "How was your appointment?" He raises his voice for me to hear over the simmering pot.

"It was a relief to talk to Dr. Gallegos, she's a good listener. I feel better about what's happening with my dreams." I look over at the back of his head and see him nod, but he doesn't attempt to look at me.

"That's good she alleviated your worries that you might be going crazy." I hear his teasing tone, which falls a little flat since he still doesn't turn to look at me.

I scoff. "I didn't think I was going crazy, but I didn't know if this was in the realm of 'normal' or if I needed to be worried about some kind of funky sleep condition."

"I know, just teasing." He turns to look at me quickly, then abruptly turns back and hunts for the TV remote.

I busy myself stirring the noodle and sauce pots.

"What did she say? Will these dreams keep happening? Is there a way to help them?" His voice is serious again.

"Oh yeah, she had helpful tips." I add salt to the sauce. "She thinks they'll go away on their own as the stressors in my life even out. But to help with that, she suggested some destressing activities to help me feel calmer, particularly before sleep. She wants me to get more exercise during the day, like taking walks on my lunch breaks, and fifteen minutes of relaxing yoga an hour before bed, and keep a dream journal. She was pleased when I told her I was already doing that last one; thank you for reminding me about that. Recurring dreams can also be caused by sleep apnea. She's going to have me tested for that in a month or two if these dreams continue. She doubts it's related but wants to rule it out."

"Those activities sound fairly easy to implement into your routine. It must be nice to have permission from a doctor to go on dream dates." The teasing words have an edge to them that I ignore. I huff again but feel myself blush. I'm glad Jeremy isn't looking at me. I pointedly turn away from him to stir the sauce, my cheeks warm. From the steam, of course.

I glance over my shoulder at Jeremy, feeling annoyed with his attitude. "Maybe if my dream journal is interesting enough, I can turn it into a lurid novel."

He jumps up then, drops the remote on the sofa, and goes back to his room.

I gape after him, wishing I'd kept my misplaced joke to myself. I don't know how to handle this situation. Jeremy is showing all the signs of jealousy, but if he won't admit feelings and persists in being upset about an imaginary man, I don't know what to do. The whole situation is ludicrous.

Jeremy doesn't reappear for dinner. Before heading out for a walk, I set a bowl of spaghetti outside his door.

The cool evening air is refreshing, and it's good to be away from the charged ambiance of the house. Maybe this walk will do more for me than just help my dreams.

The sun is setting behind the mountains, and the air is crisp and cool but not yet cold enough to require a jacket. Initially, my arms have some goosebumps, but as I work up a sweat, I no longer feel the slight bite in the air.

As I walk, I think through all the things happening in my life. Much of it feels out of my control, like I'm waiting to see what others do before I decide how I'm going to react. I'm surrounded by drama at work, at home, and while asleep. Perhaps not really while I'm asleep. If I'm being honest, these dreams with Adrian have been quite pleasant and fun. My feet rhythmically hitting the sidewalk lull the swirling emotions and thoughts in my head. The stars are starting to pop out by the time I get back home. My head feels clearer and I'm more relaxed.

Chapter 12

VALANCY

I'm sitting in the café again. Already a huge milkshake is in front of me. It's pink with red swirls of syrup around the glass, a blue-and-white striped straw, and a mountain of whipped cream.

Adrian sits down across from me.

"You didn't meet me in our usual spot in the park," I tease him.

"I don't have to meet you every time you visit, you know."

"Don't you?"

He considers this for a moment. "I'm not sure, but either way, I would want to." He smiles disarmingly, and I feel myself flush.

Suddenly changing the subject seems like a good idea. "Do you want to try some of my milkshake?"

"Absolutely." He pulls the green-and-white straw on his side to a better angle and takes a sip. "Mmm, that's tasty! I've never had that before."

"You've never had a strawberry milkshake?" I ask incredulously.

He looks resigned. "You're always surprised by these things. I've told you, the details are created by guests."

"No one's ever had a strawberry milkshake before?"

"Guess not, or they didn't share it with me."

"That's kind of sad."

He looks puzzled. "Why?"

There's no way to answer those kinds of questions. "Here, have some more." I push it nearer him, but he pushes it back to me.

"Let's both have some more." He leans over to sip on his straw and gestures for me to do the same. We share a companionable silence, enjoying the dessert.

I have an idea. "What else haven't you tried?"

"What?"

"What is it that you want to try but haven't gotten to?"

"I don't know?" He raises an eyebrow questioningly.

"Hasn't anyone ever done anything or eaten anything that you saw that you thought you'd enjoy trying but didn't get to?"

He ponders this. "Someone came once, and they had these grabby straps on their shoes instead of laces."

I blink. "Excuse me?"

"You know, you tie or buckle your shoes to keep them from falling off your feet. These shoes had these grabby, fuzzy, scrapey straps instead. Super cool-looking!" His eyes sparkle with excitement.

With a monumental effort, I contain my inner mirth. Who

am I to judge someone's fantasies? "Do you mean where one side is little loops, and the other side is tiny hooks and when you push them into each other they stick together?"

He nods delightedly.

I match his enthusiasm. "Whoa! You definitely need to try those out!"

"But I can't manifest things," Adrian responds sadly.

"I'm familiar with this product; I'll help you. Let's find a shoe store!" I take his hand and pull him outside. A light rain is falling, and the cobblestone street shimmers in the sun shower.

I see what I'm looking for. "Here we go." I lead him to a nearby shop with an antique sign depicting a boot hanging over the door. I'm hoping this appears exactly how I imagine.

We walk in, raindrops glistening on our hair, and a bell on the door tinkles invitingly. An attractive older woman with silver curls and a cozy red cardigan looks up from behind the counter and greets us with dimpled, smiling cheeks.

"Hello, dears, how can I help you?"

I take the lead. "My friend"—Adrian gapes as he looks over at me—"has heard about these awesome shoes that have hook and loop strip closures instead of laces, and he wants to try some on." I'm proud of myself for how serious I sound.

"Oh, of course! We have a wonderful selection of those types of shoes, just over here." She leads us to the back corner of the shop, where a large red ottoman sits flanked by a three-sided mirror.

After we sit down and she measures his feet, she brings out a wobbling stack of shoe boxes. The fun begins.

Adrian pulls out pair after pair of shoes. There are footwear of all styles: sneakers, Mary Janes, loafers, sandals, dress shoes, clogs, you name it. But they all have one thing in common. With each new pair, he delightedly rips the fasteners apart and puts them on his feet. I make him model them for me in front of the mirror. Some of them are so outlandish! Then he rips them apart again, giggling with joy when he hears the distinct tearing sound, removes them, and moves on to the next pair.

The rain outside has become a deluge, but we're ensconced in the shoe shop with a cozy fire in the grate and mugs of hot chocolate brought out on a tray by the store attendant. It's the coziest rainy afternoon punctuated by the delightful ripping of tiny loops and hooks. The pure joy on Adrian's face is my favorite part.

Chapter 13

ADRIAN

I can't remember ever being happier. In all my time in the scapes, no guest has ever done anything for me. I've been in this shop dozens of times, but this is the first time it has ever looked quite like this. Valancy did this for me.

I recognize the hallmarks of what she loves in the shoe shop surroundings. Everything is pleasing and appealing. The shop is quaint and cozy, with warm hues and comforting smells. It's even pouring outside, which enhances the feeling of contentment and warmth inside.

She has a marvelous sense of the esthetic. The scape looks the most beautiful I've ever seen it when she's here, and she fits perfectly into the setting she creates. I still remember the second time we met, when the bar was green and golden and her dark red hair caught the sunlight. Breathtaking. It was hard to keep myself from reaching out to touch it.

Today is the most relaxed I've ever seen her. Up until now, there has always been underlying tension and stress emanating from her, affecting the scape and her experience here. That's gone now. Now she's lounging on the ottoman with her legs tucked up under her, cradling her mug of hot chocolate. She looks completely relaxed while laughing at my antics as I model shoes for her.

Speaking of shoes, hook-and-loop shoes are the way to go! They're much easier to take on and off than having to tie them every time. What a great invention.

Finally, all the shoes Mary the saleswoman brought out have been tried on, and I flop down next to Valancy and smile. "Whew! I'm tired."

She laughs. "I bet! All that hamming it up while you were trying them on looked exhausting. It was tiring to watch." She flicks my arm to let me know she's teasing and takes a sip of her drink.

I laugh with her but then become serious. "Thank you. This was the best gift I've ever received. The *only* gift I've ever received."

She looks embarrassed but pleased. "Don't be silly, it was just some shoes."

"It was much more than that, and I think you know it. It was the first time that a guest has ever thought about me and done what *I* wanted."

She looks into my eyes. Hers are light blue with long, pale lashes, and her cheeks color again. She certainly wears her feelings on her sleeve. She looks away. "Have you ever thought about asking?" she asks.

"Asking?" I'm not sure what she means.

"There are things you want, but do you ever tell your guests that? Do you ever ask for the things you want? How are they supposed to know if you don't tell them?"

I stare at her in shock. Why haven't I ever thought of that before? I look at the fire, thinking about this. I've gotten used to Valancy surprising me, but the surprises continue to be surprising. I turn back to Valancy. She's gone.

I feel tears prick my eyes. *Sheesh, hold it together, Adrian.* Guests leave suddenly all the time. In fact, that's a hallmark quality of their departures. *Snap out of it.* I give myself a shake and pull myself together.

Mary walks over. The shop is returning to its baseline, as is Mary. She's still an older woman, but now she's wearing overalls over a floral blouse and her black hair with gray streaks is pulled back in a bun.

"That seemed fun," she says, smiling. "I wonder what inspired that specific shoe style."

I laugh and shrug without adding to her speculation. I don't want to encourage gossip about Valancy. I say goodbye and head to the door. Outside, the rain is gone and the sky is dark. I sigh, stuff my hands in my pockets, and turn for home. The puddles on the ground dissipate as I walk.

My apartment is in a typical scape tenement building for employees. It's small with one bedroom, a basic kitchen, and a den. Comfortable, but utilitarian. Because we can't manifest details, the original designs are made to be appealing and useful, if not precisely beautiful.

What I appreciate most about it is that it's mine. I control my apartment, not the guests. Guests roaming around the scape don't impact my home, or any of the other employees' living quarters. They're off limits. Guests are oblivious to them.

I flop down on the sofa and lean my head back, closing my eyes. I'm exhausted. Valancy was right; it's tiring being a fashion model. I smile at the memory.

Today was a beautiful day. I don't think I've ever had more fun. Valancy's laughing face appears in my mind's eye and I smile again, but that's followed by a sigh. This whole thing with Valancy is unusual in the extreme. I'm completely intrigued, but at the same time I'm afraid of what's to come. Why does she keep coming here, and why is it always me she meets? Are we being drawn together somehow?

I stand up and go to the kitchen, trying to distract my thoughts. I take out a preprepared dinner and start warming it up. My thoughts keep returning to Valancy. I have tons of questions bouncing around in my head, and no one to ask. Maybe I don't want to know the answers.

After dinner has settled, I go to bed early. My last waking thought is that I hope I dream about Valancy.

The sun is rising over the mountains to the east. On the west side of a small town, I'm standing on a hill. The upper branches of cottonwood trees lining the banks of a river that runs through the valley glow in the morning light. I see a path leading down from where I'm standing. It goes past a gazebo and then meanders down to a neighborhood.

I look around me. I'm alone up here, surrounded by quiet nature sounds. Desert-dwelling animals scurry about their morning errands and birds sing in the trees.

In the valley below, I see yellow school buses and white garbage trucks starting their routes. Early commuters are getting ready to merge onto the highway. Soon the bustle of the day will take over. But for now, the in-between time after the sun rises but before the day fully begins still reigns.

A small bird hops toward me. Instead of a chirp, it *pings*.

The alert startles me awake. *Is it Valancy?* I hop out of bed and run to the window. My shoulders slump. No, the scape would never appear this way if it was her. I pull my reader from my pocket and check it. Franklin is primary this time, and I'll probably be secondary or tertiary. I get ready and head to the park. I'll hang out there until I'm needed.

I swing for a time, enjoying the hordes of people milling about the park before another alert sounds, telling me where I need to go. This visitor is going to ride the wheel.

As I walk in the direction of the dive bar where Frieda works, I see the guest. She's a young girl with long, brown hair in messy braids. Her purple T-shirt has a cat with sunglasses on the front. She looks scared, and as I approach her, I feel my appearance shifting. I'm taller and skinnier than normal, and I'm wearing a sleeveless sweater with a diamond design on the front.

When I get near her, she runs over and starts pulling me in the opposite direction of the wheel. She digs her heels in to get me to move with her. I hold my ground because my purpose here has yet to be revealed. "What's wrong?" I ask.

"Daddy, I don't want to ride on the Ferris wheel."

"Okay, then we don't have to."

"But I don't want to." This is a common occurrence. It doesn't seem to matter what I say. The visitors seem to have the story already mapped out, irrespective of how I respond to them. That's one of the reasons why interacting with Valancy has been such a different experience. She talks and listens and responds to me. She changes her decisions based on my input. This girl is essentially ignoring me except for how I corroborate what she has already decided to do.

Suddenly, instead of pulling me away from the wheel, the

girl changes direction and leads me at a mad dash toward it. I'm used to this, and I'm following her lead, when Valancy's voice rings in my head. *"Have you ever thought about asking?"* Of course, she doesn't understand the logistics of this type of situation, but could I try to change the outcome?

I stop.

The little girl is straining at my hand, trying to get me to move, but since I'm much bigger than her, I'm able to stand my ground. Finally, she eases up and looks up at me.

"Why did you stop?" she asks. "We have to go to the Ferris wheel."

She's currently responding to my actions and seems aware of me. Here goes. "But you're afraid of it."

She gawks, and I feel her eyes focus on me more than they have up to this point.

"If you're afraid, why don't we do something else instead? There's a petting zoo with bunnies over there." I point to one of the least scary carnival attractions surrounding us.

She looks in the direction of my finger, and I see her body relax, the fear dissipating. She starts pulling on my hand again, this time with excited energy instead of fear. "Let's go pet the cute bunnies, Daddy!"

"That sounds like a good plan. I bet they have some fluffy ones."

The little girl is gone, and I'm idling on a swing again,

thinking about her. I didn't connect with her the way I do with Valancy, but for the first time with a random guest, I felt this was more than just a mindless job. I was heard, and I changed the interaction. More importantly, I made it better. As opposed to watching a little girl be terrified of heights, I got to hang out with a child squealing with joy surrounded by fluffy bunnies. I did something good for someone else.

Chapter 14

Running late this morning. I found it hard to shake the sleep and dream thoughts from my mind as I was getting ready, causing my shower to last longer than normal, and I savored my tea and toast at a more relaxed pace than I should have.

Everyone else's cars are in the lot when I push open the door. Daphne is sitting at the front desk. Something's amiss.

"What's wrong?" I ask.

She glances around nervously before saying in a strained voice, "Clarance has taken some actions." The last word comes out almost as a sob.

"Actions?"

She collects herself. "After you left yesterday, Mark and I asked Clarance if he wanted to go for coffee with us. He seemed nicer yesterday."

"I noticed that too."

"He said no, but that we should enjoy ourselves, so we went. Then we ran into some folks from the history center. We ended up being gone about an hour and a half."

I nod, waiting for her to go on.

"Well, we came back and it's as though he'd just been waiting for us all to not be here."

The nervousness is turning into fear. "What did he do?"

She's warming to her topic. "That bench out front that Elton sits on to greet folks. He removed it and threw it away. It's gone. Trash pickup happened this morning before we noticed it was missing."

"How dare—" My blood is boiling and then simultaneously freezing as anger and sadness build in me.

"Wait." Daphne holds up a finger. "There's more."

I stand there with my mouth hanging open, pulse pounding, as she continues.

"And then there's the matter of Peggy Leonard. Those sweet hot air balloons she makes, he decided they weren't a good fit for our brand. He called her and told her to come get them or he was going to throw them out. She called Mark at home last night—you know she's known his family forever—and tore him a new one. He didn't know what to tell her except that he was sorry."

Again, I start to vocalize my thoughts, but again she stops me. "There's more."

I feel my anger turning into defeat. "What else could he have possibly done?" I burst out.

"He's apparently done some assessment of our peak visit times, and he's decided we need to be open more hours. He rearranged our work schedules, pushed through approval with upper management, and updated them on our website." Here her voice shakes. "I didn't look at everyone's, but he made my schedule much less manageable. I don't know if it'll work with our family's babysitting arrangement." Tears well up in her eyes.

There are many things I'm willing to work with and endure and try to find solutions for, but Clarance has pushed me to my limit. He has upset Daphne, the sweetest woman to ever live, and what he has done has hurt others too. Elton doesn't show up until lunchtime, but the absence of his bench is going to be keenly felt. And I'm sure the damage to our relationship with Mrs. Leonard isn't going to be easily mended.

I square my shoulders. "Don't cry, Daphne. We'll figure out something. Where's Mark?"

She takes a breath, swallows, and nods. "He's out taking 'the longest walk ever' and we're not to expect him back anytime soon."

That's fair. "And Clarance?"

"He's in the back at his desk, I think. Mark already told him he was out of line."

"Then it should come as no surprise when he hears about it a second time."

I leave my belongings up front and storm to our office area. Clarance is sitting at his desk, his body angled uncomfortably to face as much away from the door as possible. I stomp over to his desk. I see his back stiffen as I approach.

I brace my arms on his desk, leaning toward him slightly. "How dare you!" My tone is seething. I'm not an aggressive person, and this is our workplace, but he needs to know how badly he has screwed up. I wait.

Slowly he turns around to face me. I'm rather surprised at his courage. I'm not the tallest or bulkiest woman, but I'm a spitfire when I'm angry. I can see that he's bracing for the onslaught he knows I'm about to dish out but is prepared to take it. Part of me, the part that isn't pissed, admires this about him. I would've guessed he was made of weaker stuff. His nose is slightly red, and his eyes look watery. Has he been crying? No, I note the bottle of allergy pills on his desk.

He inhales and steels himself. "What is it that you want to say to me, Valancy?"

I pause for a moment, surprised by the upfront question. What is it that I want to say? I know he has been reamed out by Mark already, and knowing Mark, he did a thorough job. Mark's a sweet and tolerant guy, until he's crossed. Then you'll definitely know he's angry with you. Clarance has surely been made aware of the repercussions of his actions. But as I think that I steam again, because when has this man demonstrated any understanding? For all I know it went in one ear and out the other.

"I'm not going to tell you again how badly you messed

up." He looks surprised. "I'm sure Mark already told you." He inclines his head in acknowledgement. "What I'm going to say is that it didn't need to be this way." His eyes widen.

"When we heard you were coming, we were apprehensive because change is hard. But we were prepared to put in a good effort to welcome you and give you every opportunity to be a valued member of our team." He looks surprised. "But you came here ready to hate us and ready to be hated."

"I don't hate—"

"Don't interrupt me." He closes his mouth abruptly. "We made efforts to include you, to adapt, to be friendly, and never once did you take any of the olive branches we offered. If you didn't prefer something, you didn't kindly say so, you had to rudely separate yourself from us." He looks down. "You screwed up yesterday. But it's more than your actions that are the issue here, it's why they happened at all. You haven't made any effort to know or understand anything to do with our culture here. You steamrolled in with the changes you decided were correct. You didn't take into consideration that we might have more insight into the value of things or that including us might matter. No one said you couldn't make changes; in fact, we expected you to and were prepared to help, but changes should've been done as a team, not by you alone. You hurt people, and you didn't have to upset anybody. If you'd talked to us, we would've given you our insight and helped you achieve your goals, even if we didn't agree with everything."

I pause to catch my breath.

Clarance grabs a tissue and blows his nose. Definitely snot and not tears.

He rolls his shoulders and stands up. Throws his pile of used tissues away and locks his computer. At last, he turns to me. His face is impassive, a mask.

"I think I'll go home for the rest of the day. Jillian may have given me her cold."

Without another word, he departs, leaving me standing with my mouth agape.

A minute later, Daphne comes back to check on me. "Why did he leave? What did you say to him."

I shrug. "He said he thinks he's coming down with his daughter's cold."

"But what did you say to him?"

"What we've all been thinking. That he's made this whole transition harder than it needed to be by being dislikable. That none of this would've happened if he'd talked to us as his colleagues."

"It's true," she agrees.

We stand there for a minute, lost in our thoughts. Finally, she looks up with a wan smile. "Let's make teas and take them to the porch. I brought some homemade sourdough."

"That's a good idea. What about Mark?"

"I texted him that Clarance left for the day. I'll leave a note on his desk to join us on the porch when he gets back."

Daphne and I are cradling hot mugs and starting to talk through the craziness that Clarance unleashed when Mark appears. He looks beaten and defeated, and his shoulders slump as he sits down in the chair next to mine. Gently, I push him back in his seat and place a piece of sourdough with butter in front of him. I nudge the mug of tea I made for him closer.

"We don't have to talk about this any more today," I say. "We're all upset. Things will get better. They have to. Let's just enjoy our tea and bread."

His shoulders relax slightly, and he takes a shuddering breath, releasing it slowly. He takes a sip of his tea, and his shoulders release a little bit more. For the next half hour, we have the idlest of conversation combined with long spans of silent sipping and chewing. We're all grieving the damage Clarance has done, but the companionship of those we trust helps. By the time it's opening time, we're feeling better prepared to face the day. It may not be a good day, but we'll get through it together.

***

I'm exhausted by the time I get home. The emotional strain of the day has worn me down. It's hard to present a pleasant front to customers when everything is crashing and burning behind the scenes. I've been looking forward to talking things through with Jeremy.

When I push the front door open, I'm reminded that Jeremy

texted this morning that his mom needed help with her house and he's going to spend the night at her place. I slump when I remember and go through the motions of putting my things away and trying to find something for dinner. I end up warming up a can of soup. I eat half but then I'm no longer hungry.

I drag myself to my bathroom and fill the tub. I sink into the warm water and let all of my emotions flood out of me. Sobs rack my body. Everything is just too much.

I was planning to do yoga this evening, but I'm too fatigued from everything. After my bath, I crawl into bed, burying my face in my teddy bear. Bob joins me in bed, probably confused because it's early for sleep, and curls up with me as the little spoon. The ache in my heart lessens as his soothing purrs and soft fur comfort me.

Chapter 15

VALANCY

I'm on a swing at the playground, going back and forth, back and forth. Leaning way back when my legs go up, all I can see is sky and upside-down buildings. It's making me seasick, but I like the feeling of the world being turned topsy turvy. I close my eyes and savor the feeling of the breeze on my bare feet and arms, my ponytail bobbing up and down with the movement and the strain of the ropes against my palms.

"Am I interrupting?"

I right myself suddenly, which is a mistake. The world spins for a minute while my equilibrium re-establishes itself. When it settles, Adrian is sitting on the swing next to mine.

"I'm glad you're here, Valancy." His smile and crinkling of his eyes corroborate this. "What did you want to do today?"

"You're usually the one with the ideas."

"That's because I know this place better than you do."

"Is there a beach?"

"No, there isn't." He looks appropriately bummed.

"Could I wish one into being?" I wheedle.

"No," he says firmly, "I don't think that's a good idea. It's best to stay within the general parameters of the scape you're in."

"That's too bad. I'm barefoot today"—I wiggle my toes—"and wading sounded fun."

His face lights up. "I have an idea! If we go that way, there's a pond." He points in the opposite direction we usually take to the city.

"A pond would be good!"

It's the tiniest pond. I'll admit I feel a little disappointed, but Adrian is clearly pleased with himself for thinking of it. I carefully control my features to hide my feelings and appear enthusiastic.

He runs over to the edge of the water and takes off his shoes and socks. He crouches down next to the water. "Oh, look! Valancy, come here, quick!" His enthusiasm is adorable as he beckons me over. I pick my way across the slippery bank and crouch down beside him. "Look there." He points at tiny orange-and-white goldfish swimming in the shallow water. They have chubby cheeks and elegant ribbon fins and tails.

"They're the sweetest fish I've ever seen," I coo as I stick a finger into the water to try and touch one. "I wish I had food to give to them."

He hands me a can of fish food and winks.

I laugh and sprinkle some near the fish. They dart about,

enjoying their snack. Adrian and I stare at them, mesmerized.

"Are you going to wade?" Adrian brings my attention back.

"Yes, I suppose that's why we're here after all, but you have to wade too. I'm not going to be the only one." I stand up and start rolling up the cuffs of my skinny jeans.

Adrian nods in acknowledgement and follows suit with the bottoms of his chinos.

Gingerly, I stick my toes in the water. "It's cold."

"Of course it's cold, you wimp." He gives me a light shove from behind, which pushes me farther in. I'm submerged up to my calves.

"Hey! Stop that!" I laugh. "If I want to be slow about wading, I can be slow, okay?"

"If you say so," he acknowledges. "But what about splashing?" He scoops up water in his hand and flings it at me, getting water on my shirt and arms. He bursts out laughing at the shocked look on my face. He starts to scoop more water, but before he can, I make the biggest wave of water I can with my foot and launch it at him. He stands there dripping, resembling a wet rat. The ringing peal of laughter coming out of my mouth turns into a scream when he lunges at me, causing water to splash everywhere. I duck and grab his waist, but he's bigger and stronger than me. He manages to outmaneuver me and dunks me instead. I emerge from the water spluttering and soaked, alternating between coughs and laughter.

We stand there sopping wet and shivering for a moment until we get control of our merriment. We're cold and wet, but happy. It's not possible to be mad at him.

"C'mon, let's get dry." He wraps his hand around my arm to help me balance on the uneven, slippery terrain, and we start to slog our way out of the pond. There is a pile of fluffy towels, dry clothes, and a small campfire waiting. We take turns changing behind a convenient fence. I wring out my hair and wrap it in a towel. Adrian rubs his head vigorously until his hair is standing on end every which way. It's fine; I'm sure his hair will dry looking perfect. Mine, on the other hand, will be a tangled mess.

We sit next to each other on a log, savoring the warmth of the fire and the comfortable feeling of dry clothes. I notice specks of light outside the ring of brightness from the fire. It takes me a moment to realize what's causing them.

"Fireflies!" I squeal, jumping up.

Adrian reels backward in surprise. "What?" he yelps.

"There are fireflies! Look at them!"

Nonplussed, he stands by the log with a bemused smile on his face as he watches me run after the elusive spots of light.

I run back over to him with my hands cupped together.

"Look," I gasp breathlessly, "I caught one!" I hold my hands out to him, separating them enough so he can peek inside at my tiny, glowing captive. His tolerantly amused expression shifts to wonder as he watches the bug light up my hand cave.

"Wow, that's amazing. I've never seen one up close before," he says reverently.

We stand like that for a minute, captivated by the tiny insect and its blinking body. Finally, I carefully release it, and its light bobs away as it joins its friends. I sigh with satisfaction. There is nothing more magical than lightning bugs.

We sit down next to each other in front of the flames again. The dancing light makes my eyes hurt; that must be why they're stinging. Couldn't be tears, not when this is such a beautiful evening.

"When I suggested a beach, this wasn't what I meant, you know," I say at last.

"This was better." He jostles my shoulder.

I nudge him back. "It was."

I'm dreading seeing Clarance today. While a small part of me hopes he didn't catch his daughter's cold, the majority of me can't help hoping that he did and stays home today. Now I feel bad for wishing him ill, literally, but I think we could all use some breathing room.

Mark's is the only car there when I arrive. I make a beeline to our office area and peep in.

"Hey, how're you doing today?" I ask.

He smiles wanly. "A little better today, I think. Talked with an old friend on the phone last night and then got a good night's sleep. Feeling more at peace with all of this. How about you?"

"I'm still upset."

He gestures in understanding.

"Is Clarance coming in today?

"He's not. He's sick. He's going to stay home today and maybe tomorrow."

My shoulders relax. "Does it make me a bad person that I'm relieved to hear that?"

He shakes his head and smiles. "Not at all. Or if it does, then I'm also a bad person. I think we can be grateful that the timing of his illness coincides serendipitously with when we all needed a break."

"You phrased that nicer than I would have." I laugh as I head to my desk.

The day proves to be a much-needed respite. We all work on our own projects. Conversation is minimal because we're busy, but the silence is genial.

After our lunches, Daphne and I take a walk. We stroll in silence initially, enjoying the sounds of traffic and kids playing at the school nearby. She breaks the silence first.

"I miss this feeling. I know it hasn't been that long since Clarance started, but he's changed things so much."

"He has," I agree. "I think I'm grieving."

"I'm sure you are. I know I am. But even with him here,

there's no reason we can't still do things like this. Let's make sure we remember to take control of what we can." She smiles hopefully at me.

"You're absolutely right. We'll have to make time to do this more intentionally." We walk on for another few buildings without saying anything.

"Do you want to hear about my dream last night?" Daphne asks eagerly.

"Sure! Was Clarance the villain?" I smirk at her.

"No, no, no! That would've made it a nightmare." She laughs. "It wasn't that exciting, but I enjoyed it. I was in a barn and when I walked out, I was on a farm. There were tons of people working, but I didn't talk to any of them. Instead, I went to the farmhouse and into the kitchen. Esteban was shelling peas or something, and I sat down and helped him. We talked about everything under the sun, the way we used to before Fred came along. Then when it got dark, we moved out to the porch and swung on the swing." She looks over at me. "It was one of those dreams that feels real, and you wake up and wish it would continue. You know what I mean?"

I nod. I know exactly what she means.

"I do know. I have an unusual dream condition, and it's been particularly exacerbated by all the Clarance stress lately."

"Oh, really? I didn't know that. Have you been having nightmares?"

"No, it's more like very vivid, real-feeling dreams. Lately they've been dreams that pick up where prior ones left off."

Daphne shudders. "Ugh! That sounds creepy."

I shrug. "I guess I'm kinda used to having atypical dreams. They aren't disconcerting when I'm in the dream. They're enjoyable. But it is odd when I wake up and have the realization of reality again. I had a doctor's appointment about it just to make sure there was nothing to be concerned about."

"That was smart of you! I bet that helped ease some of the stress."

"Yeah, it did."

In spite of the comparatively relaxing day, I notice a slight headache as we're locking up. It's even worse by the time I walk into the house. I take a painkiller.

When Jeremy gets home, he finds me curled up in my room reading in dim light to not exacerbate my headache. I look up apprehensively when he comes in.

"Hey," he says.

"Hey," I say.

Well, this is awkward.

"I wanted to say I'm sorry for how I've been acting lately," he says, not making eye contact.

I wish I had the energy to push the subject and delve into the core issues of what's happening, but even considering those things makes my head throb.

I swallow. "That's okay, there's been a lot going on lately. I understand it hasn't all been easy to deal with."

He nods and continues to stand there awkwardly. As much as I want things to be resolved between us, I really hope he isn't going to decide that now is the time. I'm not physically up for it. After an uncomfortably long pause, he finally says, "Did you want to watch some more of our show?"

I shake my head and wince. "No, I have a bad headache. I'm not going to be able to look at any bright screens tonight."

His demeanor shifts immediately to concern for me. "Are you okay? Have things been bad at work? Can I help?"

I rest my head back against the cushion. "I'm sorry, Jeremy, I'm not feeling well. I'm okay, but I don't have the energy to discuss anything. All I want is to be left alone, please."

"Oh. Of course." He starts to back out of my room. "I hope your head feels better tomorrow."

"Thanks. Have a good night."

"You too." He gives me a tiny smile and the door clicks shut. I breathe a sigh of relief and turn back to my book, but the words swim and it makes my stomach roil. I need to give up and go to bed.

Chapter 16

ADRIAN

"Where do you live?"

"What?" I look up from the cards I'm holding. I'm pleased with my hand. I usually get dealt terrible cards when I play with guests. Go figure.

"Where do you live?" she repeats.

"Oh. Um, over that way." I wave my hand vaguely. Valancy raises an eyebrow. "It's beyond the bounds of the main scape."

"So, you can't take me there?"

What is it about this woman and asking questions that makes me feel like an idiot? I know that guests don't go to the apartments, but I don't know that they can't.

"I don't know." The other eyebrow rises this time. I shrug exaggeratedly. "Really. I don't know. Guests will naturally ignore our housing, but I don't know for sure that you're forbidden to go."

"Could we try?" she cajoles. Then I see her catch herself

and backtrack. "I'm sorry. Ignore that," she says firmly, sitting back against her seat. "I forget sometimes that you're here doing a job and th-that we aren't on equal footing. Please forget I asked to impose on your personal domain." She peers resolutely at her cards and selects one to play.

I'm touched, particularly by the stammer. Valancy can be insistent, but you can tell how much she cares about respecting and caring for others. "Don't worry about that, Valancy. Being with you isn't work. We're spending time together. Trying to go to my apartment could be interesting. I don't mind; it would be nice to show you my place, and now I'm curious."

She looks up and smiles delightedly, showing rows of white teeth. There's a slight gap between two of them. "Truly?"

I throw back my head and laugh; she's incredibly easy to please. "Yes, c'mon." I stand up. "I was going to win this game anyway. I'll accept your concession."

"Now wait just a minute, mister. I have a great hand."

I laugh again, pull the cards out of her hand, and set them face down on the table. "I'm sure you do, but we can play another time. C'mon." I head to the door of the diner and hold it open for her as we exit. Outside on the street, she loops her arm through mine and sighs contentedly. I look down at her, surprised. "What is it?"

"Oh, nothing. This is nice, isn't it?" She smiles up at me.

It's the best.

When we get to the archway that leads to staff housing, I pause in front of it and look at her. "Can you see it?" I motion in the direction of the arch.

She looks puzzled but serious. "I only see a wall."

"Understandable. Hmm... let me think. I think the most likely way to succeed is for me to hold your hand while we go through, but you've got me curious, and I want to know if you can get there without me. What I think we'll try first is I'll go through, and you can see where I went, and then I'll come back out and you'll try without me."

"Do you think it could be dangerous for me?" She sounds apprehensive.

"No, the scapes are specifically designed to be safe for employees and guests. Situations may feel dire but aren't actually. I think the worst that could happen is that you leave earlier than you would've otherwise."

"That makes sense. Okay, let's try your way."

I walk through the archway and stop a few feet beyond. Before walking back out, I look at her standing there for a moment, knowing she's unable to see me. When we're together, her attention is often on me, making it hard for me to admire her without drawing attention to the fact. Valancy is a beautiful woman, but she seems mostly unaware of it. Sometimes she touches her hair or face, but mostly she seems to exist without artifice or worry about her appearance. That's less common than you might think.

She stands there, winding a curl around her fingers,

pretending at nonchalance, probably wondering where I am. I need to go back. I've delayed too long, and she's glancing around nervously. She looks vulnerable and alone. I stroll back out, and her face relaxes when she sees me materialize.

"Now I'll stay here and watch while you go through. Once you're on the other side, stop and wait for me."

Valancy squares her shoulders and walks toward the arch, which must appear as a solid brick wall to her. I admire that she doesn't flinch when she approaches it, although she does hold her hand out somewhat in front of her. She passes through and immediately turns to face me in delight, bouncing in place. I follow her eagerly, and she clutches my hand in excitement.

"It worked! I get to see your place!" She bobs up and down.

Amused by her infectious enthusiasm, I lead her down the tidy path. "It's this way."

VALANCY

The living areas for the scape are plain. Everywhere else I've been in the scape has been vibrant and colorful, with rich textures and beauty. This place is subdued and utilitarian in comparison. It's not an ugly place—the buildings have appealing lines and the palette used is a soothing blend of blues, creams, and browns—but there are no ornamentations or personal touches, aside for some manicured greenery.

Still holding my hand, Adrian leads me up a flight of stairs. I'm not sure how many times we zigzag as we proceed upward, but finally he stops in front of a medium blue door.

I like the color.

He unlocks the door and motions for me to precede him. It's cool and quiet inside and the lighting is recessed and diffused, giving the place an underwater or deep-in-a-forest feeling. It's pleasant, but as I look around, I find the space to be uninviting. Actually, "boring" is a more accurate word. My face must show my antipathy.

"You don't like it?" he asks, looking around defensively.

I relax my face into something more pleasant, but I doubt he'll be fooled. "It's lovely, but…"

"Impersonal."

I'm surprised. "Yes, exactly. Why haven't you done more with it?"

"I can't manifest change."

"Not even here in your own space?" That seems odd. "Can't you get decorative items for it from the same place you get your groceries?"

"No, I'm still built differently than you. We're not the same sort of person, in spite of how we appear. And I don't think a trendy display of toilet paper would add much."

Typically, shops sell more than disposables, but if he can't, he can't.

"Interesting. May I look around more?"

He motions for me to go ahead, and I proceed to inspect the rooms. His home is small but comfortable. In keeping with the rest of the housing complex, it's also the same tasteful palette of blues, creams, and browns. Aside from the utter lack of personalization, there's no fault to be found. It's comfortable, practical, and soothing. It sets the hairs on the back of my neck on end, but I can acknowledge it's simply my own bias making me uncomfortable. This isn't a place where I would want to live, but there isn't anything wrong with it. It's simply a culture I don't understand.

I walk back into the living room, where Adrian is perched nervously on the edge of the sofa. "It's pleasant, Adrian. I'm sorry my initial response seemed negative. It's just different than what I'm used to. I have an idea, though."

His eyes twinkle. "Why am I not surprised?"

"Could I try to manifest something for you here?"

"Guests can't manifest here."

"How can you be sure? You said no guest has ever been here before." If I was a meaner person, I would probably take great pleasure in discomfiting Adrian as often as possible. As it is, it happens frequently enough without trying that I struggle not to laugh. This man has clearly never questioned anything about his existence before meeting me.

"I mean, I suppose I don't really know." He looks uncomfortable with this new train of thought. "I guess you could try. Why do you want to make something here? I like it how it is. If you succeed, do you think you'll be able to remove it after you're done?"

My heart sinks. I've been impulsive and thoughtless again. "I apologize, you misunderstand me," I explain hurriedly. "I'm sorry if I've made you uncomfortable. I would never presume to change your home. The reason I asked is because you don't have any personal touches here, and maybe I could help with that, if that's something you would value. Maybe together we could make something that you'd appreciate having here."

His shoulders relax, and I could kick myself for flying off halfcocked and forgetting how my meaning could be misinterpreted. It's completely ingrained in him to do what visitors want. Even here in his private domain, it's an underlying assumption.

"I've always wanted personal touches. What would we make?"

I'm relieved to see genuine interest in his eyes; he's not agreeing simply to please me.

"Why don't we try something small and simple. Something easy for me to understand and imagine. I don't want to accidentally cause something awful to show up." We share a knowing look, remembering the tea party-and-bull fiasco.

He thinks for a moment before looking up. "What about a shelf on the wall in view of the sofa? Something attractive in its own right that can also be used to display things."

"What sorts of things are you going to display? Toilet paper?" I tease.

He considers this dilemma. "Maybe that's not such a good idea. Oh! I know! Could you make a wooden sign similar to the one that was hanging outside the shoe shop, but instead have it say something pleasant on it? And instead of having it stick outward on a metal bracket, have it hanging flush against the wall."

As I picture it in my mind's eye, it feels like a reasonable choice. "I think that'll work. Now, walk me through what I need to do again." I don't want to do something incorrect.

"What are you trying to create?" he asks.

"I want a wall artwork that's made of wood. It should have smooth, curving edges and the words 'Welcome Home' etched on it in blue letters," I say with intention.

He smiles and nods. "Where do you want it to be?"

"I want it to be on this wall"—I point—"just above eye level. I also want it to be pleasing to the eye but simple in design. It should complement the color scheme and décor of this apartment."

"Anything else?" he asks.

"No? How long do you think it'll take to appear?"

He shrugs. "Who knows? It may never, but we will have tried. That was a good idea."

"Should we try another one?"

He shakes his head. "No, I think that's enough. If it doesn't work well, then it's only the one failed attempt. I can always hang a towel over it if it's terrible." He winks at me.

That sounds sensible. I move over to the sofa and sit down

beside him. I feel uncomfortable now that I don't have a purpose here. In the scape, there is always something to do. Here I'm at loose ends, sitting in the silence of Adrian's apartment.

"What do you want to do now?" Adrian asks, leaning his head against the back of the couch, his eyes watching me.

"I didn't think very far ahead on this one. I think I thought the scape would continue to shift wherever I was, presenting all sorts of new opportunities. It's not the same here, and I'm not sure what to do now."

"It is different here." He sounds pleased by this fact. Maybe he finds the predictable a relief compared to his ever-shifting work environment.

"You mentioned that you've worked in other scapes. Have you lived in those scapes too?"

"I've always lived here. I pass through the arch, and it takes me to the scape I currently work in. And when I look out the window, the view is my current scape. If I get assigned to another scape, the arch will take me there and my view will change, but my apartment will stay the same."

"What about your neighbors?"

"They see whatever scape they work in and pass through the arch the same way."

"How many people work in the scapes? This place doesn't seem that big."

"There are vast numbers of employees. They all live here,

and you can always find who you're looking for, but there must be some kind of condensing process in place to make it visually manageable. I'm sure the massive amount of housing needed for all of us would be overwhelming to navigate."

"I don't think I'll ever understand."

He chuckles. "I think that may be the point."

Now it's my turn to be taken aback. I stand up abruptly. "I think we should go back to the scape."

He pushes himself upright. "Are you all right?" His hand reaches out to me.

"Yes, I'm fine, but I don't think I belong here." I feel a wave of sadness as I say that. It hurts to realize that the person I am is fundamentally at odds with this place. Not because I care about spending time in Adrian's apartment, but because that means Adrian and I are incompatible too. I look at him and see his expression is atypically blank.

"Okay, let's go back," he says. His tone is almost harsh.

As we head back to the arch, I take in as much as I can of all that surrounds me. Everything is both plausible and implausible. Normal hallways and staircases branch off from each other, but there's no way I could ever find my way without a guide.

As we approach the entry arch, which I can see clearly from this side, Adrian leans over and wraps his arm around my shoulders, pulling my body sideways into his in a half-hug. "Thank you for asking to see my home. It means a great deal to me that you asked."

I look up at him. "Thank you for showing it to me. I'm sorry if I acted weird at the end."

He squeezes my shoulder and clears his throat. "You weren't weird, I promise." He smiles shyly at me.

I feel my cheeks heating, and I take a step away. "So," I say quickly, "should we do it the same way as last time? You watch me go through?"

"Naw, we know it works now. We can go back through together. C'mon!" He takes my hand, clearly unaware of the electric charge that shoots up my arm, and leads me through the arch. We pass under the shade of the arch and the sunlight from my bedroom window greets me on the other side.

Chapter 17

VALANCY

I roll over and my head aches. The light filtering past my curtains makes my head hurt worse. Bright knives of light stab me. I flop over the other way, which makes me cough. Great, I'm sick. I must have caught the bug from Clarance.

ADRIAN

Standing at the archway, suddenly at loose ends, I contemplate what to do with the rest of my day. I'm close to home, of course, but I don't feel like calling it a day just yet. I stuff my hands in my pockets and start to walk aimlessly. I can still feel her warmth on my body.

VALANCY

I text Mark to let him know I'm feeling sick and am taking the day off. There's no issue, but I always feel half guilty when I miss work to take care of myself.

Next I text Jeremy so he knows what's going on. He checks on me before leaving for work. "Is there anything you need before I go?" He stands awkwardly next to my bed, staring down at me.

I shake my head. Ow. "No, I'm all right," I croak. "I'll just have a lazy day. Have a good day at work."

He looks unconvinced. He returns a few minutes later with a glass of water and box of tissues, which he sets on my bedside table. He gives a quick wave, and I hear him leave the house.

I lie snuggled in bed, with a second pillow propping up my head and Bob curled at my side. I'll get up eventually, but for now I'm comfortable and exhausted. The game I'm playing on my phone has a lulling effect and soon I feel my eyes droop.

ADRIAN

The effect Valancy has on the scape has almost dissipated by the time I get near the bar. As I'm pushing on the door to go in, I start to notice vibrant details returning. The paint on the door is now bright teal and the handle is shiny brass. That's odd. What the heck is happening?

I feel a ping. Is she back already? I look at the screen. *Dang it, Valancy, did you really have to show up on the other side of the town?* My sarcastic thoughts are in opposition to the excited thumping of my heart.

I'm standing at the overlook railing by the Ferris wheel. A sweet-smelling breeze is rolling across the hillside, caressing my face. My long, auburn curls are flowing out behind me. I inhale deeply.

Eager footsteps approach behind me, but they stop before they get to me. After a moment, I look over my shoulder and find Adrian watching me.

"It's easier to converse if you walk all the way up to me," I tease.

"You looked so beautiful with your hair blowing in the wind, I just had to stop and admire. I hope you don't mind too much," he teases back.

I giggle; sometimes he's perfectly charming. "When you put it like that, I can't be mad. What are we doing today?"

His expression is odd, but he doesn't say what he's thinking.

"We could ride the swings; you haven't done that before. Does that sound fun?"

"Yes! This breeze feels heavenly. I'd love to have even more blowing past me."

"C'mon, then." He reaches out his hand to me. He's always grabbing my hand to lead me somewhere. But then he pulls it back and instead beckons for me to follow him. He turns and I jog to catch up to him, slipping my hand in his. He looks down at me, surprised. I smile up at him. He says nothing but smiles back, his eyes soft.

The chair ride is farther into the city than the wheel. After it lifts you up, you fly in circles above the rooftops. I get a yellow chair, and Adrian gets a green one adjacent to mine.

Heights aren't my favorite. Even though I'm not afraid of them, they make me uneasy. I let out a squeal when my feet leave the ground, my long, blue skirt billowing around me in the draft. I hold on tight to my support chains and look over at Adrian, who is laughing at me. Infuriating man.

We're above the height of the nearest buildings. There is a brief pause when we reach the top and the whole city is spread out below and around us. I saw it before from the wheel, but this is different. Now we're within the city instead of to the side. I can see floral curtains rippling in windows, a cat skulking along a drainpipe, smoke wafting from a chimney. From here I can see that the city is alive. I wonder if it is, though, or if it only appears that way to me because it's what I desire.

Before I can spend much time thinking about existential dilemmas, the chairs start to spin. I lightly scream again, and I hear Adrian laughing and whooping. The chairs dip and bound in great arching movements. The wind whips by, twining my hair into snarled tendrils, I'm sure, but the feeling is completely glorious. I take deep, satisfied breaths of air. With my eyes still closed, I take the deepest breath yet and wake up in a coughing fit.

And she's gone again. The swings slow and I get off feeling a little dizzy, I walk to the railing where she was looking at the view. For a moment I imagine her there, her hair and skirt furling out behind her.

I wonder if she'll be back soon. Briefly, I speculate about why we perceive everything so differently. We exist here together, but we're not the same. This is just a place where we can simultaneously exist. When she came back just now, she didn't seem to realize that she'd only left a few minutes earlier. What's a continuous experience for me are discrete events for her. We don't experience time the same way.

Normally, I'm not very curious and just accept that there are truths about existence I'll never understand. But I briefly allow myself to wonder where Valancy goes when she's not with me. Does she go to other scapes, or is she somewhere else entirely?

I sit up in bed and hack for a good minute. Finally, I get enough of my lung capacity back to reach for my water cup. Ugh, that was a terrible way to wake up.

I get up, careful not to wake Bob, and go to the bathroom and stare at myself in the mirror. This isn't my best look. There is something morbidly satisfying about looking at myself when I'm sick and a complete mess. My hair is all snarls around my head and looks more reddish-orange than normal against my pale, clammy skin. I was glad when my hair darkened to auburn as I got older. I don't miss being a coppery redhead. My eyes are watering, my nose is red, and there are purple shadows under my eyes. My pajamas are rumpled and a size too big, making my braless figure look completely shapeless and frumpy. For a moment, I let myself wallow in self-pity that comes easily when I'm feeling out of sorts. Then I giggle because it's so melodramatic. I know I'll look cute again soon.

According to the clock on the counter, I've been asleep over two hours. On cue, my stomach grumbles. I pad into the kitchen to make an herbal tea with lemon and four slices of buttered toast. I get my fluffiest blanket and curl up on the sofa with my comfort sustenance. I turn on a cheesy romcom I love to rewatch when I'm sick. I know the plot by heart. Even if I stop concentrating on it, I won't miss a thing.

By late morning, this cold is kicking my butt, and I decide to head back to bed to rest more comfortably. I take more painkiller, get a hot pack for my back and another box of tissues, and shuffle back to bed. My eyes are sore. I lie there with my eyes closed instead of playing my game. My thoughts drift around feverishly, finally fixating on my earlier dream with Adrian on the swings. I wish I was as beautiful in real life as I am in my dreams. This cold is bringing out all the self-pity. Swinging in the fresh air would be infinitely nicer than lying here feeling disgusting and hot.

The swings swirl so quickly that everything stationary goes by in a dizzying rainbow blur. It's making me feel sick. I close my eyes and rest my spinning head on the chain.

"Are you okay?" Adrian hollers at me.

I shake my head without opening my eyes.

"Val, look at me!" he yells.

I shake my head, that's a definite no.

"Valancy!" My name gets carried away on the wind.

Finally, I look over at him distrustfully with only one eye open. He motions for me to look around. Carefully, I lift my head and open both eyes. The crazy onslaught of color has stopped and we're going at a speed that allows for observation of all that's passing by. I relax, glad that everything has stopped gyrating.

"Is that better?" he asks, sounding concerned.

"Yes, much." I smile at him gratefully although I don't think he had anything to do with it. The sunset is warm against my back and the shadows are long. As we go past buildings, our distorted silhouettes with legs hanging down leap over the colorful walls.

"Valancy." Adrian's voice is pitched low, but I still hear him. I look over. He has his hand stretched out to me. The look in his eyes is unfathomable. I lean over to reach out to him, and our hands clasp tightly. The force of the other's swing pulls us off course a bit, making us laugh.

I can't imagine anything more perfect than spinning and dipping and swooshing past this colorful world while holding Adrian's hand.

I spend the rest of the day in bed, dozing and dreaming and getting up occasionally for snacks and the bathroom. Curled up at my side for much of the day, Bob does a good job keeping an eye on me. My dreams are all over the place. Sometimes I'm riding the chairs with Adrian, but often I'm slogging my way through fever-fueled nightmares.

By the time Jeremy gets home with a pizza in hand, I've passed the worst of it. I'm sure I'll be sick the whole weekend, but I'm feeling less awful.

"You look terrible," Jeremy says when I walk into the kitchen wrapped in a blanket. The concern in his eyes belays the joke in his words.

"Thanks, I tried," I say sarcastically. "Actually, despite how I look, I'm feeling better. I slept most of the day."

"Did you dream about Adrian?" he asks while grabbing plates out of the cabinet.

"Some. I don't know if you've experienced this with your dreams, but when I'm sick, my dreams can be crazy. I think I dreamed about all sorts of wild stuff. I remember spinning with Adrian."

"Spinning?" He pours me a glass of apple juice.

"I think it was a swing ride."

"Ah, spinning makes sense, then." He places my food in front of me.

"Thanks for bringing me pizza. This is what I've been craving all day." I take a big bite of pepperoni, grease dribbling down my chin.

"Of course. I figured you might enjoy that." He hands me a napkin, which I use to wipe my chin and then my nose. "I'm glad you're feeling less terrible."

"Me too. Maybe I'll take a bath after this and put on fresh pajamas."

"That would definitely help make you look less like a zombie," he says seriously.

I kick him under the table with my slipper.

"Ow!" He laughs.

***

If I dreamed last night, I don't remember it. Just as well, it probably would've been one of those manic, illness-crazed dreams that is more horrifying than being awake all night. My headache has reduced to a dull pressure and the only other symptom I have is a stuffy nose. I certainly felt worse yesterday. I'm grateful it's the weekend because I need another day to recuperate.

The painting I've been working on is propped on my easel. I haven't looked at it in a few days. I arrange it to take advantage of the morning sunlight and evaluate it.

Maybe it's because my brain is foggy and sick and weird, but for the first time looking at it I see the similarities between it and the place I go in my dreams with Adrian. There is a skyline with a Ferris wheel in the background. That's interesting, because I know I started working on this artwork before these dreams began.

Actually, Val-girl, that's not weird at all, since these dreams are in your head. The voice in my head is snarky today.

Now that I've made the connection, it's hard to unsee. It

also makes me more dissatisfied with the artwork because it's not anywhere close to as magical as the scape. I'm straining my brain to try and recall details I could add to it, but it's hard to remember. If only I had better recall of the dreams I have with Adrian.

Wait a minute! I reach for the journal on my bedside table. I've been sporadically writing in it but also adding things as I have flashes of recollection. I flip through the pages and end up sitting on the floor, reliving these moments.

Jeremy pokes his head in later to check on me and seems surprised to see me on the floor.

"How're you feeling today?"

"Dot too bad," I reply stuffily. "Just codgested."

"I'm glad you're feeling better."

"Be too."

He looks like he's considering leaving the conversation there, but his curiosity gets the better of him. "What are you doing?" he asks.

Let's pretend for a minute that all my words aren't coming out very nasalized. Take my word for it, I'm hard to understand due to all the buildup in my nose.

"I realized that this artwork"—I gesture to my easel—"is a scene from the scape where Adrian lives." Jeremy looks uncomfortable, but I continue. He asked. This is who I am. "I was looking at it, thinking it seemed incomplete, and realized I have this handy dandy dream journal." I wave the journal in the air. "So, I've been reading through it and taking notes on descriptions I've included so I can make this piece feel more authentic to the scape."

"Are you just going to do this piece?" Jeremy asks, stepping farther into my room to inspect it. "It's a beautiful place."

This gives me pause. I don't typically think too much about my art, just making what feels right in the moment and finding connections between pieces after the fact. But I could intentionally pursue a series of artworks about the scape; I certainly have enough material. I've been thorough in my dream journal, and my imagination can fill in what I can't recollect… from my imagination… I catch myself in an existential quandary and force my thoughts back to the situation at hand.

"Maybe. I hadn't thought about it before. I'll see how I feel about it when this piece is complete."

Jeremy nods. "Makes sense."

Does it? Of course that's just an expression, but "making sense" seems far from the dream life I'm currently experiencing.

Jeremy must detect that my thoughts keep getting distracted. He clears his throat awkwardly. "Glad you're feeling better and moving ahead with projects again."

I smile at him as he leaves, closing the door gently behind him. Turning back to the journal, I lose myself again in my dreams and art.

By evening, I'm feeling much more myself. Tomorrow will be

another lazy day, but I'm sure I'll be back at work on Monday. I take a steamy shower and have an herbal tea before bed. I'm feeling cozy and content and much less sick as I snuggle beneath the covers.

I heard Jeremy moving about the house throughout the day, but aside from a few near collisions in the kitchen, we haven't interacted much since this morning. I'm glad there has been a good reason to avoid each other. It has given me time to think. Tomorrow, when I'm less disgusting and my head is clearer, maybe I can finally talk to him more. About important stuff. You know, the stuff you keep giving me pointed looks about.

Chapter 18

ADRIAN

I'm wandering though the city trying to figure out what I want to do for lunch. A visitor is here somewhere, but I'm not directly involved with their visit. The weather is dreary and rainy. I pull my jacket's collar higher around my neck and consider my options. Nothing's appealing. Clearly, this guest isn't in a benevolent mood. Maybe lunch is best skipped today.

I slog in the direction of the amusement park, which is unfortunately defunct. In retrospect, that should have been obvious. It doesn't lift my mood as I'd hoped. The swings look gray and abandoned, a far cry from how they looked when Valancy and I swung on them.

I sit on a bench overlooking the view and watch the mist rolling in over the green-gray hills. The copses of dark trees and patches of purple heather lend mystery and somberness to the view. It might not be my favorite, but it isn't bad to look at and it suits my mood. I slouch down on the bench, pulling my jacket tighter around me.

"Mind if I sit down?"

I jump and look over. It's Frieda from the bar, the waitress who always serves us when Valancy visits. She and I have only talked briefly in passing.

"Sure, go ahead." I scooch over on the bench.

She sits down, pulling her cardigan snuggly around herself, and we stare at the foggy landscape.

"I've seen worse," she says after a minute.

"Definitely." Another pause. "The guest isn't going to your bar?"

"Guess not. I heard they're obsessed with finding a bathroom, and my door was locked when they tried it."

"Ah." Figures.

Finally, she turns to me. "What's up with that woman I keep seeing you with?"

I continue looking at the view. "What do you mean?" I glance at her surreptitiously; she's looking at her lap.

"Why does she keep coming? I don't remember ever seeing a long-term repeat person before."

I shrug and raise my hands, palms up. "I don't know. It's a first for me too."

"Hey, at least she's nice." She smiles. "And I appreciate her taste. The scape looks great when she's here. So cozy."

She won't get any disagreement from me.

"How long before she leaves for good, do you think?" Frieda asks.

"I don't know." An ache forms in the pit of my stomach. I feel her eyes on me, questioning. I don't look over.

"Will you miss her?" she asks softly.

It feels as though she punched me in the gut. Now I look over at her and I see her eyebrows draw together as she notices the pain etched on my face.

"Oh, I'm prying into something I don't understand. I didn't mean anything by it. I'm sure I'd get attached to a repeat visitor too if they spent as much time with me as she spends with you. I'm sorry. I hope she gets to visit for a long time. I enjoy her visits too."

Frieda stands abruptly, pats my shoulder awkwardly, and heads back toward the city. I cover my eyes with my hand and take a shuddering breath. She has made me think about things I've been avoiding, but which have been lurking near the surface of my mind. Up until now, I've been enjoying spending time with Valancy, pretending it will last forever, a gift of joy I don't question. But Frieda's correct. Someday, this is going to end. It hit me near the end of Valancy's visit to my apartment that we're not destined to have a future together.

I sit there for a long time, watching the swirling mist until my swirling thoughts calm. At some point, I doze off.

The hard plastic booth of the restaurant isn't very comfortable. It looks like this place used to be a chain fast-food joint and got repurposed as a mom-and-pop place. I wonder what kind of food they serve. The window paint says "zaim ed sallitrot." Not very helpful.

An employee brings a red plastic tray of food over to me. I thank them and look down. Ah, tacos, my favorite.

Before I have a chance to take a bite, a car pulls up to the spot directly outside my window. The glare from their windshield makes me squint.

Sunlight stabbing through my eyelids wakes me up. As I rub my eyes and look around, I see glittering candy sparkling everywhere. She's back.

I'm in the park. The sunset makes long shadows of the trees. Children are laughing happily as they play. I stroll down a path, past adults sitting on benches, watching the kids.

I look around for Adrian. He always seems to catch me unawares, although I know he's not deliberately sneaking up on me. It's unusual that he hasn't found me yet.

As I head in the direction of the bar we've gone to a few times, I see him jogging in my direction. I feel my face light up, my speed increases, and I hold my hands out to him.

He takes them as he pants, "I'm so sorry. I lost track of time. Fell asleep."

"You fell asleep? Wow, you must not have been very eager to see me." I'm teasing, of course, and start to pull my hands away, but he holds onto them, drawing my eyes up to his face.

"I'm always eager to see you, Valancy. Always."

I want to look away, but I can't. I smile at him shyly. "I love seeing you too." There is a pause as we continue to stare at each other, saying things with our eyes that our voices haven't found the words for.

I clear my throat. "Would you like to get a treat?" I quirk an eyebrow.

He closes his eyes and tips his head forward until his forehead touches mine. He exhales softly. "I would love that." He pulls away and the moment is gone. "Food sounds great. I didn't have lunch." He turns toward town and formally offers his elbow to me. "Shall we go to our usual destination, madam?"

I ceremoniously take his arm and pick up the edge of my polka-dotted, knee-length skirt. "Of course, good sir, lead on!"

Dinner was wonderful. We laughed together, sat in companionable silence, and said more than we spoke. Only the crumbs of dessert remain, and we've been silent for several minutes. I've been aimlessly admiring the art on the walls, and Adrian has been inspecting his fingernails. The candle in the center of our table flickers invitingly.

Adrian looks up, his eyes dark pools in the dim light. "Would you like to join me on the rooftop of one of the skyscrapers? The view is spectacular."

"That sounds lovely."

We walk out of the bar, and I see that darkness has fallen. I pause.

"What's wrong?" he asks.

"It's night. It's never been night when I've been here."

He shrugs. "You wanted it to be night. Just like you wanted it to rain when we went shoe shopping." He looks around. "It's nice, though, almost as pretty as your sunsets. I like your change of ambiance."

He's right, it's gorgeous. The darkness is velvety purple and blue, with yellow pockets of light from streetlamps illuminating warm-toned cobblestones and fall leaves. The stars are twinkling.

"It's all right for things to change," he says quietly, near my ear.

I gaze up at him, not sure if he's referring to the time of day or something else. He holds his hand out to me, and I take it. His hand is firm and strong around mine. We stroll through the streets, warm currents of air blowing orange and crimson leaves around us. 1940s jazz music drifts down to us from a radio in someone's apartment. It's a little awkward having my feelings translated so obviously for everyone to see. For once, I'm jealous of Adrian's inability to change this world. He gets to keep his privacy, whereas I'm on display. The whole scape is a Valancy mood ring.

We go into the lobby of a skyscraper and take the elevator to the roof. Immediately, I run to the edge of the observation deck to look at the view. It *is* spectacular. Part of the city had been beneath us when we rode the swings, but now all of it is. I can see the park and the shops and the bar. The Ferris wheel is rotating slowly, with all its bulbs illuminated. People riding it are dark silhouettes against the warm glow on the gondolas. In another direction, I see the darker oval of the little goldfish pond.

Adrian walks up beside me and rests his elbows on the railing next to mine. We stand that way for a long time. My shoulder bumps against his as I'm looking around, and I leave it touching him. He doesn't move away.

"Look over there." He points with his other hand.

I look at the glow growing behind the mountain ranges in the distance. What is it? I watch for a minute until the full moon starts to crest behind the peaks. I gasp. It's enormous. I watch its progress until it's fully risen above the tops of the hills, its glow reflecting off the rippling water of the dark pond.

"Adrian." I turn to him. He's so close, and I put a hand on his chest, trying to prevent myself from falling into him, involuntarily curling my fingers around the leather lapel of his jacket.

He reaches his hand up and grasps mine. "Valancy."

His voice is tender. Whatever I was going to say is gone from my mind. All I can think about is how he's looking at me.

"Adrian, I—"

"Whatever it is, it can wait." He bends his head toward mine, and my eyes flutter closed. The last thing I see are his eyes with their long lashes closing too as he leans in. His lips are soft on mine. For a moment, it's the lightest of tender kisses, but then my arms draw up around his neck, pulling drawing him closer to me. The hair at the base of his neck caresses the skin on my hands. His arms wrap around me firmly.

When he pulls away at last, I stand there for a moment with my eyes closed. He chuckles and draws me back against him.

My eyes open a crack, and I realize I'm lying in my bed. No, no, no. I want to go back! I try to hang onto the moment, to remember the feeling of his kiss on my lips, but it's too late. I'm waking up.

ADRIAN

I stand on the top of the skyscraper feeling cold and alone, my arms empty. The soft, warm night is returning to cool baseline darkness. The ambiance Valancy added is quickly dissipating. I'm used to sudden departures, but this one is hard. Valancy left a void, not only in my arms, but also in my heart.

Chapter 19

VALANCY

Today hasn't been a good day. Contrarily, it has also been sort of magical. I'm all confused inside. It's like when you have an amazing dream and wake up and reality comes screaming back. Then the rest of the day, you're reliving those perfect moments while also fighting with the reasonable side of yourself that's telling you it was simply a dream. It's like that. Exactly like that.

I can argue with myself until I'm blue in the face that Adrian is only a figment of my imagination, but today he feels like more. This is why vivid dreams can be unsettling.

I'm so conflicted. It sounds crazy to even be comparing the two, but having Jeremy in the real world and Adrian in my dreams is just impossible to reconcile in my mind today. At some point in my internal monologuing, I tell myself I deserve some grace. I didn't create this situation, at least not consciously, and it's okay for me to not know all the answers.

I spend most of the day resting; I want to be fully recovered for work tomorrow. I work on my painting some more, start reading a book I've been meaning to open for the past three months, and play the silly phone game I'm currently addicted to. However, I do make a point of not taking a nap. I can't delay sleep forever, but I don't want to invite extra opportunities to dream right now. I need some distance from my dreams.

Jeremy's at home again today. He typically has a lot of activities planned for his weekends, and I can't help wondering if his presence here is because I've been sick. Maybe he cancelled his plans to make sure I'm doing okay? We're not spending time together, but I feel his comforting presence in the house.

I wanted to talk to him today. To call him out for his reticence and aloofness and try to get to the heart of the feelings I'm certain we're circling around. Even if I'm wrong, I think that getting things out in the open will be healing for both of us. Right now, we're stuck because there are too many unsaid things and feelings.

But because of my dream—and my kiss with Adrian last night—my mind is all muddled up. Jeremy hasn't been receptive to my dream situation lately. I don't know what to do. I don't think I can explain what's happening in my dreams with indifference, and I don't know if Jeremy can handle that.

He brings me a grilled cheese sandwich and homemade lemonade for lunch because I got completely absorbed in my artwork and lost track of time. He sets them on the table next to my messy paint palette.

I didn't hear him come in. "You're my favorite!" I exclaim. My response is less tempered than it might have been if he hadn't caught me by surprise.

He blushes. "You're welcome." He purposefully looks at my painting. "Wow, this piece is turning out amazing."

"Thanks! I found my groove with it, eventually."

"You'd mentioned that, but I hadn't thought to ask to see it. That's awesome! I know you're in the zone, but I wanted to remind you about taking a walk after you eat. Not trying to manage your health situation for you, but I thought maybe the reminder wouldn't be misplaced since you've been sick and that messes up habits."

"Aw, thanks for keeping me on track, I appreciate that. I *should* do that," I say as he's turning to leave. "Hey, Jeremy?"

"Yeah?" He turns back to look at me. I think I see hopefulness in his expression.

"Do you want to come with me? We could climb part way up the hill to the lookout point." Our neighborhood is adjacent to a nature reserve with a sizeable hill. About halfway up, there is a plateaued area with a gazebo.

There's a moment of hesitation. As I've been considering this situation with Jeremy, I've begun to realize that his strange behaviors seems to be stemming from an effort to hold himself back, like he's specifically avoiding situations where he's close to me. But I've also noticed he's not very good at actually keeping himself from doing things he really wants to do. I hope he won't be able to resist.

"I'd love to."

"A bit before sunset? Maybe, like, five forty-five?"

"Sure."

After Jeremy leaves, Bob jumps down from the window with a purry meow to inspect my lunch and beg for a bite. His entreaties are hard to resist and soon, he's savoring a blob of melted cheese. I scratch the little white spot under his chin and tease his tail as I think about taking a walk with Jeremy later. Maybe this will be the opportunity I've been waiting for.

Despite my best efforts to not pre-stress and worry about our impending walk, I feel my pulse thrumming in anticipation when I meet Jeremy on the front porch.

The air is currently warm, but I know the temperatures are going to drop quickly in the desert. I'm wearing jeans and a graphic T-shirt with a hoodie wrapped around my waist. I don't want to have a chill when I'm still borderline recovering from being sick. Jeremy minds the cold less than I do, and his only concession to the possibility of cooler temps is that his T-shirt is long-sleeved.

As we head down the path, walking abreast, a breeze kicks up, blowing my hair into my face.

"Bleh! Just a second!" I yelp.

Jeremy stops to watch with amusement as I bunch my hair unceremoniously on top of my head and wrap a scrunchy around it. I'm definitely not winning any style contests tonight.

The first part of our walk is through the neighborhood. We don't live that far from the neighborhood we grew up in, but not close enough to walk to. I feel a slight pang as I think nostalgically about our childhood park and the good times we shared there growing up.

"Do you ever go to our park?" I ask, breaking the silence.

Jeremy glances over at me. "The one in our parents' neighborhood?"

"Yeah."

He shrugs. "Not really. My mom dragged me to a community picnic there one time when I was over at her house. Aside from that, I can't remember the last time I went there. I guess it was probably with you." He smiles fondly at me. "Maybe we should go back sometime together and see what's changed."

"Do you think there would still be tadpoles?" I ask eagerly.

He laughs, throwing his head back, his Adam's apple bobbing. "You were *obsessed* with those pollywogs. I just thought they were kinda cool and made the mistake of introducing you to them. Then every year, we had to monitor their progress, count their numbers, protect them from predators." He teases me. I know he enjoyed our tadpole adventures.

"Whatever, Jeremy. I recall you coming to my house one time super early to tell me there was a cat hanging around the pond. You insisted we go back and protect the tadpoles. You were invested too!"

He shakes his head in denial, a grin spreading across his face.

"You were!" I giggle, poking him in the ribs.

He laughs, grabbing my waist and tickling me.

I shriek and dodge away from him, holding my hands up in surrender. Jeremy is the worst tickler, and I never stand a chance against him.

He accepts my capitulation, and I bump his arm with my shoulder as we continue on. He bumps mine back, careful not to throw me too much off balance since he's a lot bigger than me. I savor the feeling of easy companionship, the lightness in our interaction that I haven't felt in a long time. The sun is low in the sky, and the shadows from the houses we pass are long.

We reach the edge of the neighborhood, and Jeremy steps to the side to let me pass first through the gate. I'm a slow hiker on an upward incline; it has always been our custom that I go first to set the pace. He follows a few steps behind me.

The hill is sparsely covered with low tumbleweed and sagebrush shrubs. The sun is still hitting some areas, and insects hum and buzz around. The dimming light is also prompting some wildlife to explore. We see a jackrabbit loping away and Jeremy points out a family of quail dodging through the shrubbery.

No one else is hiking. We're near a big subdivision, but the only sounds I hear are those of the wind, the wildlife, and our feet upon the sandy path. It's lovely. Since we met, Jeremy has always been my person, the one I feel like I can be myself fully with, who appreciates and likes me just the way I am. I'm glad for this moment together. Whatever happens, I do feel secure in the knowledge that our friendship will survive; we'll always at least have this.

We reach the gazebo just as the sun dips below the horizon. Supposedly, you can see the green flash at sunset in the desert, but I've never seen it. I watch hopefully for it anyway. Alas.

The sky will still be bright for at least forty-five minutes; we have some time to enjoy the view before we need to head back.

We stand together, silently gazing out at our hometown below us. Landmarks pop up above the houses and trees that we've known forever: the water tower, the courthouse, a church steeple, the lights of our high school football field. It has always been magical to look down on things here instead of seeing them from the normal vantage point below. Seeing the bigger picture and how they all look together solidifies them as elements that work together to make our town whole.

The breeze is starting to have a nip to it. I untie my hoodie and pull it over my head, messing up my haphazard bun. I undo it all and retie it in a ponytail, since the wind is blowing away from my face up here.

Now that I've got myself situated, maybe it's time to address the elephant in the room. Or on this hill, I suppose would be more accurate. I turn toward Jeremy.

He turns to me at the same time and says, "I'm sorry again for not being supportive of what's happening with your dreams lately."

That wasn't precisely how I was going to start this conversation, but it'll do.

I clear my throat. "That's something I've been wanting to talk to you about, actually."

His attention is focused on me. The breeze ruffles his hair a bit.

"I've been feeling very conflicted about a lot of things that are going on in my life right now." He nods.

"My life is all over the place. I'm having these crazy dreams and work has been a nightmare, and you're tiptoeing around me, which makes me feel like I can't talk about all the things that are bothering me with the one person I would normally seek out to share with."

His eyes drop and his shoulders sag.

I take a step forward and reach out a hand to rest it on his shoulder.

He looks at me in surprise.

"Don't feel bad. I think I understand."

"I doubt that," he scoffs.

"Jere, we've been friends forever. Do you think I'm so obtuse I can't read between the lines? Something has changed with how you feel about me, hasn't it?"

There's a long pause. He gazes into my eyes, for once not looking away. At last he nods. The confirmation of what I've suspected surprises me more than I thought it would.

I gasp and involuntarily step back from him. He still doesn't break eye contact with me.

"I don't know when things changed for me," he says. "It was a few months ago that I really noticed. One day we were cooking in the kitchen and teasing each other while making breakfast on the weekend, and it just hit me that this was what I wanted the rest of my life to be like. That being with you is what makes my life perfect. You've always brought so much joy to my life.

"But then I realized what I was feeling was one-sided. Just because I feel that way, it doesn't mean you could ever feel the same in return. That's what scared me and why I've been so closed off the past few months. I didn't want you to know how I felt. I didn't want to be the cause of our friendship dying. Because even if we couldn't be together, being your friend is still the second best. I couldn't risk losing that." He continues to hold eye contact with me. The pain in his eyes is clearly visible; this has been hard for him.

"I understand."

"How could you possibly understand, Valancy?" His pent-up emotions burst out in frustration. "You've been oblivious until recently, living your life, falling in love with some dream guy, pursuing your art. I've always been just this supportive friend in your life. How could you understand what I've been going through?"

I know he doesn't know what he's saying, but it hurts to hear his condemnation. Tears spring to my eyes and I turn away from him, away from the view.

"I understand, Jeremy, because I've been doing the same thing for years. I've been in love with you since you were dating Natalie."

"Wait, what?" He grabs my shoulders and turns me to face him. "Since Natalie?" He's shocked. "That was a decade ago."

I nod, feeling the tears pool. "It's been longer than that."

"Oh God, Valancy, I didn't know. I'm such a jerk." He pulls me into a hug and wraps his arms around me, resting his head against the top of mine. I cling to him, willing myself not to cry, but feeling such relief that everything is finally out in the open.

"No, you're not. I didn't want you to know," I mumble into his chest.

When we finally break apart, we stand there awkwardly, looking and then not looking at each other. We could compete with teenagers for "most awkward pseudo-romantic encounter." Neither of us breaks the silence. There is still so much I think needs to be said, but I don't know where to start. I look out at the view again and see that it's getting dark.

"We should head back," I say. "It'll be too dark soon."

He looks at the sky in surprise, then follows me back down the hill.

We're silent on the walk back. I appreciate having time to absorb what just happened. Part of me is thrilled, part of me is terrified, and another part is unsure exactly how to move forward. I wonder what Jeremy is thinking about.

We get back to the house and each split off to our own rooms. I change into a comfortable lounge outfit and brush my hair free of all the tangles the wind and my haphazard ministrations added. I go to the kitchen and start boiling water for tea.

Jeremy comes in a few minutes later.

"Would you like a tea?"

"Sure, thanks." He sits down at the table. He looks exhausted.

I join him with mugs and set one down in front of him before sitting in my spot. I blow on my tea, stalling for time.

"There were other things I wanted to talk to you about tonight," I say after a minute.

"Oh?" He looks at me questioningly, his hands wrapped around his cup.

"I did want to push this"—I gesture between us—"thing to a point where we could talk about it. Thank you for helping me do that. It's good to not have secrets anymore."

He nods.

"But as I said earlier, my life has been wild lately. And something you said on the hill wasn't far from the truth."

Jeremy looks uneasy, not sure where I'm going with this.

"You said I was falling in love with some dream guy." I pause here, holding out the idea. Jeremy stares at me and swallows hard, but doesn't say anything.

I continue. "I've wanted to talk to you about these dreams with Adrian, but you haven't handled the idea of him very well. Each time I dream about him, it's like the story with him continues. I know it sounds outrageous, but I've gotten to know him as a person."

"Valancy—"

"I know, I know! Believe me, I know. He's in my head. He's imaginary, but in my dreams he feels real. And when I'm there, I can't remember anything about the real world or you or anything about myself. I'm just there having adventures with him. It's only when I wake up that I can see the whole picture."

Jeremy looks concerned. "So, what are you saying?"

I take a breath. "What I'm saying is that I'm currently dealing with an unprecedented situation, and I don't know what to do about it. I did call Dr. Gallegos again and told her what was happening. She says that I still don't need to be concerned, but to keep doing the steps we discussed to try and get the dreams to resolve on their own. I'm not worried that I'm losing my mind or anything, but I'm still conflicted."

"Conflicted how?"

"It's hard for me to reconcile all the emotions I'm feeling. I stress about the situation with Clarance, have feelings for you in the real world, and then have feelings for Adrian when I'm asleep. I'm thrilled, you have no idea how much, that you and I are finally being honest with each other about how we feel, but I don't think I can move forward even thinking about that until my dream situation improves. It's not fair to you or me to put us through that sort of emotional roller coaster. Please tell me you understand."

Jeremy pushes his chair back and comes over to me. He leans over and wraps his arms around me. "Of course I understand." He rubs my back soothingly. "Not about the dreams, or how they feel, but I understand what you're asking of me."

I think I feel him kiss the top of my head and for just a second, I let myself sink into his warmth and scent, breathing in the peace I feel with him.

He releases me and goes back to his seat. He reaches his hand out to me and I grab it tightly.

"I'm here for you, Valancy. I always have been and I always will be. I've always known you have an insane dream life, and this is just part of that. I think the idea of a romantic guy in your dreams frustrated me a lot more before because I couldn't tell you how I felt. But now you... we... know what's happening between us. I can wait, Val, for however long you need to figure things out."

I jump out of my seat and throw my arms around his neck. "Thank you, Jeremy, you're the best."

He awkwardly hugs me back, laughing. "I know." He yelps when I poke him hard in the side with my finger.

Chapter 20
ADRIAN

I'm just emerging from the housing complex when my pager pings. Even before I look at it, I know it's Valancy. The air is taking on a brisk crispness, there is a faint, chilly breeze, and drifts of yellow, orange, and red leaves line the cobblestone street. I think I see a pumpkin in a window as I hurry toward the pond.

I see her before she sees me. She's near the water, wearing shoes this time, carefully peering into the depths. Two ducks swim on the side farthest from her, and colorful, drifting leaves congregate near the edges of the water. Her hair is in a braid down her back and she's wearing a long, lavender dress with a ruffle along the bottom hem. The purple stands out against the warm tones of her surroundings. I smile. She's always a feast for the eyes.

She straightens when she hears me approaching and pulls me in for a hug. I wrap my arms around her and smell cinnamon. Finally, I pull away from her.

"I-I'm s-sorry." I stumble over the words and thoughts that are rushing around in my head.

"What are you sorry for?" she asks kindly, smiling up at me.

I shake my head. "I don't know."

She reaches her hand up and places it on my bicep. "What's wrong?" She looks concerned.

"Nothing." Argh! "Everything!" I turn away from her. I glance back at her and see that the smile has fallen off her face.

"Come on, let's take a walk." She takes my left hand in her right and then wraps her left farther up around my arm, leaning her head against my shoulder. Our feet crunch through the leaves. I'm starting to feel cold; I think the weather has gotten cooler. I glance down at her and see she has a dark purple cardigan over her dress now. I wonder if she has noticed.

We don't say anything for a long time. It's nice to be together, mostly alone. A few people are out and about, but most seem to have gone inside, where it's probably warmer. When we get to the playground, I stop and turn to her.

"I think what's upsetting me," I say, "is that I'm afraid there's no future for this"—I wave my hand through the air between us—"and that makes me unbelievably sad."

Her eyebrows pull up in the middle and her chin trembles a tiny bit. She looks away from me, toward the city. "That does seem likely." She turns back to me. "Why would we be the exception to the rule?"

I shake my head in agreement. What we have is unprecedented, which is what makes me think it's almost certainly fleeting. A beautiful anomaly.

"But hey..." She pats my shoulder. "We're here today, like this, and it's lovely, right? Like, could anything be more lovely?"

I smile at her; I can't help it. "Nothing. Every day with you is perfect."

She smirks. "I'm not sure that could possibly be true, but I do love spending time with you as well."

"It's true in my world," I say.

Her face contorts a bit.

I've seen that expression before. "What is it?" I ask.

"It's like there's something just barely out of reach in my mind. I'm not always here, clearly, because you experience long gaps where I'm absent. But I don't know where I am when I'm not here."

"And that probably is the fundamental crux of why we can't be together." I pull her into my arms, and she rests her head on my chest. "We only overlap a little bit, and I think we're probably going to see that shift. This won't last forever."

She leans back and looks up at me. "Well, then let's make the most of the time we have left." She takes my hand and drags me into a side street I don't think I've been down with her before. I let her lead me through a grungy glass door. The first thing I see are tables for two and four along the edge of a dim room. A disco ball rotates slowly above a wooden dance floor, and a country-western band is playing a melancholy song.

I look at her in surprise; this isn't her typical hallmark style. "What is this place?" I ask.

"A place to dance," she replies. She pulls me to the center of the empty dance floor. "Do you like to dance?" she asks, maybe considering for the first time that dancing is a mutual endeavor.

"With you, of course." The music changes to a two-step, and I take her hand in mine, placing the other behind her shoulder blade. She rests her hand above my collarbone, and we begin to move to the music. We gaze into each other's eyes as we dance. I pull her closer to me and spin her out, she wraps her arm around my waist as I spin the opposite direction, and we come back together, laughing. No other couples join us. We have all the space we could ever want, but I enjoy holding her close and watching her twirl away, the ends of our fingers keeping us connected. I wish this song would go on forever.

Finally, the music slows, and I give her one final slow spin. When she comes back to me, she stands on her tiptoes and plants a sweet kiss on my cheek.

Clarance and I are back at work. We've strategically placed tissue boxes on our desks, but otherwise there is no acknowledgement of our mutual weekend of suffering. If he was Mark or Daphne, we would have teased each other about the importance of keeping germs to ourselves. But it's Clarance. There's no companionable interaction, and teasing is a dirty word.

I'm sitting up front in the morning, which is great since it means I can avoid Clarance. I'm somewhat morosely plunking away on my computer when Elton comes in. I look up as the bells tinkle and I'm instantly saddened. He looks upset.

"Hello, Mr. Burrows," I say, since "good morning" doesn't seem appropriate.

"Hi, Ms. Val. I, um. My, um…" He looks around, trying to figure out what to say.

"Your bench is gone."

"Yes." He sounds relieved. "Do you know where it is?"

Why is this my responsibility? This isn't my fault. Is this the first time he has been here since his bench was removed? I clear my throat. "A decision was made to remove it."

He looks horrified. "*You* decided this, Ms. Val?"

I'm devastated he thinks for a second that I could do such a thing to him.

"Absolutely not, Elton. I would never do something like that. I know how special it is for you to sit out front. People love coming here to visit with you."

"Then who did it?" His voice is heated; he looks livid.

As much as I long to let him loose on Clarance, I feel a loyalty to The Paint Palette and feel compelled to present a united front even when I disagree with choices that were made. "It was a decision made by higher-ups because the bench was getting old, and the paint was looking shabby."

He nods, his anger gone as fast as it appeared. Now he simply looks deflated. He, too, knows the futility of arguing against the ephemeral 'upper management.' "Will they put in a new bench?"

"I'm not sure. That would be nice, but it's not my decision to make. I can pass the idea along." A glimmer of hope surfaces in my mind. Maybe Clarance would consider a replacement.

"Well… thank you, Ms. Val. I-I guess I'll go to the park."

My heart feels heavy. "Okay, Elton, I hope you have a good day." I cringe at the words I say automatically.

The bells sound flat as the door closes behind him. I sigh as the sound fades away and turn back to my work. That's when I see Clarance standing in the archway. My blood boils when I see him.

"It shouldn't have fallen to me to tell him. I'm not in the habit of breaking hearts, and I don't appreciate being made to do someone else's dirty work."

I glare at him and he opens his mouth to reply, but before he can, I storm out of the room. I go out to the patio and sit down. I'll only be gone a few minutes, but I need a moment to get my feelings under control. Hopefully, Clarance will have gone back to his desk by the time I come back inside.

A couple minutes later, when I've taken some deep breaths and feel myself calm down, I go back in. Mark is sitting at the front desk, scrolling on his phone.

"Hey, what's wrong?" he asks, looking up from his screen.

"I've had better mornings. Elton came in for the first time since his bench disappeared. That wasn't fun."

Mark frowns sympathetically. "I'm sorry it ended up being you who had to tell him. I would've told him if I'd known when he was going to come in."

"I know you would have, but really, it should've been Clarance who told him. He's the one who made this mess."

Mark nods, ruefully.

"Where is he, by the way?"

"He came back to my office a few minutes ago and asked if I could come up front. He said he needed to run an errand and that you'd stepped out for a little while."

"Huh, I wonder where he went?"

Mark shrugs.

When Clarance comes back an hour and a half later, he acknowledges me only with a chin lift and proceeds back to our office area. Avoiding conversation with him is a boon. I debate asking him about getting a new bench, but I'm still too angry. I won't present my case well today.

In the evening, I'm curled up on the sofa when Jeremy comes home. I've been nervous about seeing him after all that transpired yesterday, but he seems to have embraced the idea of waiting for me to let him know when I'm ready for our relationship to change. His tone and manner seem normal. All that's different is the lack of reserve that has been a constant presence the past several months.

"How did you feel today?" he asks.

"Better, some nose blowing. Clarance"—I roll my eyes—"was congested too. Pity that's the only thing we have in common." I flop back against a pillow, feeling frustrated.

Jeremy comes over and sits on the opposite end of the couch. "I guess I don't know very much about what's been going on with him. I haven't been a very good listener. Do you want to tell me about it?"

It's wonderful feeling good talking to Jeremy again. It hurt my heart when I felt like he wasn't someone I could really talk to anymore. We chat a long time about everything that has happened with Clarance, and I feel so much better getting his insight and encouragement.

"Would you like to be my plus one to Mr. Hampton's reception on Saturday?" I ask, after talking through all the work drama. I feel myself flush.

"Are you asking me on a date?" Jeremy looks shocked and places his hand demurely on his chest.

He's ridiculous. "No, silly, I'm asking you to come help us set up the event. You can do all the heavy lifting for me." I wink at him.

He looks offended. "I see. You just want me for my body." I slap him playfully and don't respond to his insinuation. He becomes more serious. "Of course I'll come with you. I'm interested in meeting this Clarance fellow and it'll be nice to see Daphne and Mark again." Jeremy has stopped by The Palette a few times.

"Awesome!"

"I know I am."

I swat him again.

I get to bed at a good time, and I feel cozy. You know how sometimes your sheets and the air conditioner, and your pajamas are all in zen with each other and it's just the best feeling? I sigh contentedly as I scrunch my toes against the blanket. Bob hops up next to me and after circling a few times, he nestles against my chest and stomach. I drape my arm over him, finding a position that is comfortable but doesn't rest too much weight on him. I fall asleep listening to his murmuring purrs.

At the foot of the Ferris wheel, the view of the confection hills is gorgeous. This is my favorite place to look at the view because the buildings don't get in the way or detract from the vast, glittering landscape.

"How many?"

I start and turn toward the ticket attendant who's waiting for my response. "Sorry, two please." I assume Adrian will be here soon.

They hand me two red tickets with gold foil accents, and I step over to the fence to wait for Adrian. Where is he?

Of course, she had to show up right when I'd sat down to eat and wasn't properly dressed. I dash out of my apartment and fumble for my key, causing it to fall into a topiary next to my door. Blast! I jog down the stairs and collide with a neighbor on a landing, causing her to spill her groceries. I seriously consider leaving her to pick everything up by herself, but I'm just not that type of person. By the time I get to the archway, I'm sprinting. Valancy must be wondering why I'm taking so long.

I see her by the wheel, and a smile breaks out on her face when she sees me approaching.

There he is. Poor guy, he looks harried. Maybe I arrived at an inconvenient time. I reach out my hands to him as he approaches, excited to be in his arms again. Just as he gets to me, everything goes black.

 ADRIAN

If she'd vanished in a puff of smoke, I couldn't have been more surprised. The tickets that were in her hand flutter listlessly to the ground and vanish. My heart stutters as I see everything reverting.

Has it started to happen already?

 VALANCY

I climb the stairs to the second level of the commuter train car and find a forward-facing seat with a table. Slinging my bag onto the empty seat next to me, I settle in for the ride to Santa Fe.

The countryside rushes by, trees and farms and houses darting in and out of view. Occasionally, I catch a glimpse of something magical, like a calf racing the train, a scarecrow in a field of corn, or people hiking down a dry arroyo. I dig through my bag and pull out my art supplies to sketch.

I regain consciousness slowly. My dream was so pleasant, I want to hang onto it. I can still feel the vibration of the train around me, making my sketches a little wonky. Riding the train is so soothing. I burrow deeper into my covers, ignoring the light creeping around the edges of my curtains. My alarm hasn't gone off yet, but it won't be long before it does.

I contemplate what I can recall of my dream and reach for my dream journal. Wait. This wasn't an Adrian dream. I pull my arm back under the warm blanket. I feel Bob adjust himself behind me. Did I dream about Adrian last night? I can't recall.

My alarm goes off and I fumble for my phone. I take a breath, steeling myself for the day ahead.

***

Work proceeds relatively uneventfully. There is an underlying tension, but all four of us come to work, do our tasks, and go home. Pleasant interactions are minimal, but there is no open hostility. Sometimes, I think it would be nice if we all had a shouting match. The tense politeness wears on my nerves, and I feel dread each morning when I come back.

A few customers come in and complain about Elton's bench removal, but Mark or Daphne are up front when this happens, and I'm spared these interactions. Daphne looks strained, but she hasn't again mentioned the scheduling fiasco. Judging by her body language, I'm sure she's still worried about it, but she's keeping it to herself.

Mercifully, Clarance has been running in and out on errands, preparing for Bryce Hampton's reception on Saturday. I think he's deliberately getting himself out of the gallery as often as he can to avoid us. Seems like a smart move to me, since we're not exactly showering him with attempted friendliness anymore.

In contrast, time at home with Jeremy has taken on a new sweetness that was never there before.

He still interacts with me minimally in the morning, wise man, but I've caught him looking at me shyly and smiling when he thinks I'm not paying attention.

He's giving me the space and time I asked for, but having things out in the open has changed our dynamic. There are small changes beginning to creep into our routine. We sit next to each other on the sofa while watching our show. Not touching, but not separated by the entire couch anymore. He also does little nice things for me without asking. Yesterday, I found a bag of gummy bears sitting near my tea supplies. It's sweet, but not overwhelming, his way of saying, "Here. This is how I've always wanted to act around you but was afraid to before."

We haven't talked much about my dreams lately. There's not much to discuss. The dream side of my life seems to be going back to normal. I think I've seen Adrian a bit, but mostly what I recollect when I wake up are perfectly routine dreams that have nothing to do with him. Part of me, probably the unconscious part, is sad to see the end of Adrian, but most of me is glad to not be torn by this unsettling dream love triangle I'd concocted for myself. Jeremy was right. Love triangles aren't all they're cracked up to be.

Chapter 21

I'm sitting outside at a sidewalk café, shaded by a striped umbrella, when Adrian pulls out the spindly chair across from me. He takes my outstretched hand and smiles, but there is a sadness there I haven't seen before. He also looks tired around the eyes, as though he hasn't been sleeping well.

"What's the matter?" I ask, placing my other hand on top of the one I'm holding.

"You haven't visited as often lately or stayed as long." His mouth flexes as though in pain. He waves his free hand abstractedly. "I might be imagining what I think is happening."

"You probably aren't. Something is changing."

He nods roughly, putting his other hand on top of mine. Our hands are now clasped together on the middle of the table. He opens his mouth to speak as the waiter walks up.

"Can I get you both anything?"

"No, nothing," he says.

At the same time I say, "A slice of cake, please, with two forks."

The waiter leaves with my order, and Adrian stares down at our clasped hands. He looks upset. "I'd hoped we'd have more time."

I release my hand and reach out and touch his cheek. There really isn't anything to say.

He takes a breath. "I haven't been sleeping well. I've been… upset."

I nod sympathetically. "I understand, truly."

We sit silently for a minute, lost in our thoughts.

"I love cake." I say with a grin.

Adrian gives me a quizzical look. "Okay? I guess it's good you ordered some, then."

"You have to share it with me, though."

"Duh." He narrows his eyes, looking faintly amused.

"We need to celebrate."

"That's the last thing I feel like doing, Valancy." Adrian looks at me despondently.

"I know, darling, but something special happened to us. From the first time we met, you said this was different."

He nods.

"I don't know why this happened, but it's been amazing. And while we know that something is changing beyond our control, we should acknowledge that what we've experienced is worth celebrating. This has been wonderful, hasn't it?"

"Yes." Adrian looks deeply into my eyes. "It's the best thing that's ever happened to me."

"So, I ordered cake. I want to commemorate this magical, implausible thing we've shared. And share one more dessert with you."

The waiter comes out with a quadruple layered carrot cake slice with an orange-and-green frosting carrot on top. He places it between us. I pick up my fork. Adrian looks at me apprehensively. I smile encouragingly, and he reluctantly picks up his fork as well.

"Adrian Vagary, I want to thank you from the bottom of my heart for showing me this scape. It has been a tremendous experience. But most importantly, thank you for showing me you. For opening your world and your heart to me. I know you were just doing your job at first, but you let it become much more. The adventures we've had have been both sweet and magical." I take a bite of carrot cake. It's divine.

I'm touched. My eyes sting as Valancy motions for me to have a bite of cake. Willing my hand not to shake, I take a small piece. By golly, I must make a point of eating more desserts. I swallow and clear my throat.

"Val-valancy," I stammer. I clear my throat again and she smiles at me with the sweetest, most encouraging look. God, I'm going to miss this woman. "This scape has been my workplace and my home for a long time. I've come here innumerable times with visitors who cast their own lens on everything. I thought I'd seen it in every possible mood. Then you came. When you're here, I always know it before I see you, because the scape never looks more gorgeous than when you're working your magic on it. The attention to small, beautiful details, the colors, the aura, the smells and sounds and tastes." I gesture to the cake. "Everything is wonderful when you're here, more than wonderful, and that's how you make me feel too.

"I told you when you first started coming here that I could be whoever you wanted me to be. But you never once changed me. You let me be exactly who I am and liked me for me.

"You make me see the world differently. You make me want to interact with it joyfully. You make me laugh. I've never laughed as often or as fully before. I've waited for your visits with eager anticipation, and I fear their absence because I'm afraid the joy in my life will go with you. But you're also right, this thing we found together was worth it. Whether it lasts or not, it has been amazing."

Her eyes are shimmering brightly by the time I'm done, but she smiles gamely and takes another bite of cake, not breaking eye contact with me. Staunchly, we continue to eat the cake until it's all gone.

"Shall we go?" she asks, once our plate is clean.

I nod and we head down the street together. I reach for her hand, and she gives it to me. Her skin is warm against mine, and we cling firmly to each other. We walk out to the bench I fell asleep on a while ago and we sit down, not saying anything. There is nothing left to say; we already know. Words won't change how we feel or the outcome we can't control. What's more important is that we enjoy this time we have left in our mutual understanding.

I think the peace that surrounds us lulls me, or maybe it's this bench. I drift off and when I wake up, night has fallen and Valancy is gone.

Chapter 22

VALANCY

On Friday, I leave the house earlier than normal. Last night was unusually restful, and I'm feeling invigorated. My feelings about work haven't changed, but I still feel brighter. Maybe it's because the situation with Jeremy is good and not adding to my stress anymore. I stop at Sammy's Bakery on the way and pick up some bran muffins. It has been over a week since any of us have brought in morning treats. I even get one for Clarance. He's not forgiven, but I won't withhold morning calories if he wants them.

When I pull into The Palette, only Clarance's SUV is ahead of me. Great. I pick up the muffins and my purse and head to the front door. My hand is resting on the door handle when I glance to my right and my mouth falls open.

There's a bench.

It's not the same as the old bench, of course, but it's nice in its own way. It's new, varnished wood, and whoever made it burned some floral designs into the corners of the back and seat panels. It's esthetically pleasing and fresh-looking. Seeing it, I begrudgingly agree that it looks nicer than the old one, while still fitting with the curb appeal of The Paint Palette.

I wonder who brought it. Probably one of Elton's fan club patrons who was mad at us for removing the old bench. This one does look much nicer; maybe Clarance will let it stay. I give it one more perusal and head inside.

The front desk is empty. Clarance must be sitting in the back. I peek around the door to see. He looks up, and I dart back, feeling like a small child who was caught spying.

"Valancy? Was that you?" he asks.

I take a breath and walk in briskly, pretending I'm not acting strange. Definitely not. I smile brightly. "Yes, sorry, I dropped something." That was a lame excuse. I place the muffins and my purse on the desk. "Did you, um, see the new bench?"

"Yes, I did," Clarance replies, looking at his computer screen.

"Do you think it looks good?" I ask hesitantly. "It looks more professional than the old one; maybe we could keep this one?"

He pauses what he's doing on his computer and turns his body to face me. "I certainly was planning to keep this one, since I ordered it from a local artisan to replace the old one." He waits for me to absorb this.

I feel myself flush. "Oh," is all I manage to say.

He continues to look at me expectantly.

I'm annoyed he has caught me off guard, surprised that he's the one who bought the bench, and ridiculously pleased that the situation has been resolved. All of the emotions at once are making it hard for me to articulate my thoughts. I look around for anything to prompt my tongue and see the box of muffins on my desk. I clear my throat. "I, uh, got bran muffins for everyone. If you want one, they'll be on the counter." I notice his cheeks flushing and a faint smile on his face as I duck into the kitchenette.

Hurriedly, I make a tea and take it and my muffin out to the patio. My emotions are still all over the place. This is the first time since meeting Clarance that I haven't disliked him. I don't know how to act around him when he isn't being underhanded and rude.

While I'm on the patio, I get a text from Mark that he's caught in traffic from a bad accident. That must be why Daphne hasn't arrived yet either; they take a similar route.

The patio door squeaks, and I jump. Clarance carefully closes the door behind himself and brings his muffin and tomato juice over to the table. He sits in the chair farthest from me, but his body faces mine, and there's no indication of avoidance or discomfort.

"Thank you for the muffin," he says, as he breaks off a piece. "It was kind of you to bring me one, especially since I know you haven't been pleased with me. I can eat bran muffins." He glances at me and gives a nervous smile.

"You're welcome." I pause. "Thank you for getting another bench for Elton. It will mean a great deal to him, and to all of us."

He busies himself with the paper on his muffin as a blush creeps up his neck. "I shouldn't have thrown the old one away without talking to you guys. I didn't know it had a special purpose. I just thought it was old and unsightly, and The Paint Palette would look nicer without it."

I nod and return to my muffin. I don't know what to say. Clarance as a reasonable human being is confusing for me. I'm still not thrilled with him and the other things he did, but maybe there is hope for him after all. Acknowledging mistakes is a huge step in the right direction.

We sit in slightly awkward silence, eating our muffins and sipping our beverages, until Mark and Daphne come out. They seem surprised to see Clarance, but when they find out the new bench was his doing, the atmosphere warms up considerably and they regale us all with stories of terrible drivers trying to get past the accident when traffic was completely blocked. As I sit here with my team, for the first time in a month, I believe the future at The Palette might be all right after all.

I rub my eyes sleepily and look around. Straw pokes me in the back and as I roll into a sitting position, I see that I'm in an animal stall. Morning sunlight streams through the open barn doors and I hear shouts from outside.

Standing up, I dust myself off. My heavy skirt and boots look the worse for wear, but my blue tunic seems clean enough. I walk out into the barnyard, where farmhands are running after sheep, corralling them for sheering. Everyone ignores me, and I head toward the farmhouse.

The rows of plants in the kitchen garden behind the back porch sway heavily in the breeze. The ripe crops are bright yellow, orange, red, and green. I pick a plump tomato from a vine and climb the stairs to the porch. The door squeaks as I enter the kitchen.

A woman is at the sink, washing dishes. She looks up when I walk in and smiles. It's my mother. I place the tomato on the sideboard and kiss her cheek.

"Hi, Mom."

"Hey, honey, could you chop up the vegetables?"

"Of course." I turn back to the counter with its pile of tomatoes, carrots, and cucumbers and begin dicing them. My mom hums a familiar lullaby and I join in.

Later, the stream of farm workers coming in for lunch fills the dining area. Fresh vegetable salads are placed in front of them, and I keep dicing vegetables in anticipation of more folks.

"Here, honey." My mom hands me an apron to keep me tidy.

Everyone leaves after they're done eating, and my mom and I clean the table. No one ate their salads. I snack on vegetable bits as we clear dishes. When we're done, we go out to the front porch and sit on the swing. She puts her arm around me, and I lean my head against hers. As the sun sets and the stars come out, I turn to her.

"I've missed you."

"I miss you too."

It has been a long time since my mom passed away, and my memory of her has faded and warped with time. I'm not sure if what I recollect is accurate, or if my mind has painted my memories of her more rosily than she really was. In the time directly after she died, she was in my dreams often, but as time has passed, she has appeared less and less frequently. That hasn't upset me, but in the rare times she now appears, I treasure those moments. For a brief interlude, I get to make new memories with her.

Saturday morning is peaceful. I feel relaxed and happy, still thinking about the dream with my mom. I'm working on my painting when Jeremy pokes his head in, still looking groggy.

"Hey," he says.

I swivel my stool to face him. "Good morning, sleepyhead."

He smiles sleepily. "How'd you sleep?"

"Good! I dreamed about my mom."

"Oh, awesome!" He wakes up more. "I know you love when those happen. No Adrian dreams?" He no longer sounds upset when he mentions Adrian.

I'm stunned for a second. I haven't thought about Adrian at all. "Oh… no, no dreams with him."

"What's wrong?" Jeremy walks over to me. He's wearing an old T-shirt and plaid pajama pants that look distractingly attractive on him.

"Nothing, everything is fine. Things are feeling better all around. It just threw me off that I hadn't even thought about Adrian. That's the first time in weeks that he hasn't been close to the front of my thoughts."

"The doctor did say you'd stop dreaming about him when your life evened out more."

It feels like the air got knocked out of me. "Yes, that's what I've been waiting to happen. And things are improving. I told you Clarance was fine, maybe even pleasant yesterday."

"Yes, I'm glad that situation is resolving." He tips my chin up so I look at him. "Val, it's good to stop dreaming about Adrian. I know I'm biased, but it does mean things are getting better in here." He taps my temple lightly with his finger.

I nod. He's right, but I feel dejected all the same.

"But it's also okay to be sad that it's ending. He's someone you've grown to care about; this transition may be hard."

I feel tears well in my eyes, and I wrap my arms around his waist.

"Thank you. I think it's going to be difficult."

He strokes my hair. I know it's still a tangled mess from sleep.

He doesn't seem to mind. "You're welcome. Let me know you if you need a shoulder to cry on or a willing ear. I'm here for you."

I squeeze my arms tighter around him, listening to the comforting sound of his heartbeat.

After he leaves and I turn back to my artwork, my thoughts are soothed by the cathartic meditation that making art is for me. I circle back to the dream about my mom, remembering how nice it was to spend time with her in such a peaceful setting.

Suddenly, an idea pops into my head, but I quickly dismiss it. *Don't be insane, Valancy. That farmhouse isn't a scape Daphne and I both visited in our dreams.* I laugh ruefully at myself. This dream drama has gotten out of hand if I start thinking dreamscapes are real.

Chapter 23

VALANCY

My second load of laundry is running, and I'm working on a sudoku puzzle in the living room when Jeremy rushes in looking a little frantic, holding several clothing items on hangers. "Val, what am I supposed to wear to this reception? Is it fancy?"

I giggle at his panic. "It's not really fancy, but a button-down and nice jeans or dressier pants wouldn't be out of place. Those you have there will work fine."

"Oh, good." His shoulders and face relax. "What color are you wearing and when do we leave?"

"Aww, are you going to try and match me? That's sweet." I giggle again when he blushes and put him out of his misery. "I'm wearing blue and gray. We should probably leave in about forty-five minutes. I need to arrive a little early."

"That works for me. Do you want to get food beforehand?"

"I had a snack already, and we'll have refreshments at the

event. If we're still hungry afterward, we can grab something on the way home. Or maybe ice cream?"

"I'd love that." He grins at me.

"Also, thanks for coming with me. Not that I need backup, but it'll be nice to have you there."

"It's my pleasure."

A zing runs down my spine.

***

I'm pleased with the outfit I've chosen for Bryce's reception. His artworks are colorful, so I've opted for the opposite. I'm wearing a dark gray pencil skirt that hugs my curves perfectly, navy heels that are tall enough to look cute but short enough not to kill my feet if I'm standing for a while, and a navy cowl neck blouse. The string of pearls around my neck brings the whole outfit together in a classy way. I give myself one more cursory glance in The Palette's bathroom mirror and pull a curling strand of hair over my shoulder. I look good.

I head out onto the floor to see what help is needed. Mark and Daphne hadn't arrived yet when we got here. I saw Clarance's car as we came in, but I dipped into the restroom before seeing him.

Walking into the Main Gallery, I see Clarance bending over a speaker in the corner. Jeremy is standing nearby looking like he's considering asking Clarance if he needs help. I head in their direction. Clarance stands up as I approach, and I have a moment of surprise as I realize he looks nice. He's wearing black dress pants and shoes and a dark red, button-down shirt. Red features heavily in Bryce's work; it's a thoughtful color choice on Clarance's part. He has forgone his trademark sweater vest, and I think it's an improvement.

"You look fancy!" I exclaim as I approach. "The red is a good color to complement Bryce's show." He looks self-conscious, looking down at himself, and I think I detect his ears turning red. I can certainly empathize with his blush-susceptible skin. He seems at a loss for words. I press on to rescue him from what apparently is an awkward compliment. "What help do you need from me, or us?" I deliberately look around the room to give him a moment to collect himself. I make eye contact with Jeremy and his eyes twinkle.

Clarance clears his throat and says in his pleasantest tone to date, "I have the snack items in the break room refrigerator. Mark said there were serving dishes, but I couldn't find them. Can you tell me where they're kept?"

"Oh yes, Mark keeps them in a box on top of the fridge since we don't use them often. Do you want us to get them cleaned up and put the food on them?"

He nods, briefly acknowledges Jeremy's existence, and mumbles, "That'd be helpful." He turns back to crouch in front of the speaker, and I get the impression that we've been dismissed. Surprisingly, this time I'm not offended. Clarance is acting different, almost pleasant and normal, if I'm being honest. Maybe not to my standard for normal, since he's still painfully awkward, but the rudeness I've come to expect is gone. I can accept some social awkwardness. It's a huge improvement from where we were. I motion for Jeremy to follow me.

Back in the kitchenette, we start working on the food. Clarance has bought some nicer items than we typically get: gourmet meats and cheeses, petit fours, and roasted vegetables, to name a few. Jeremy gets to work cleaning the dishes I set out, and I dry them and attractively arrange the hors d'oeuvres.

Mark touches base briefly when he comes in and then goes to help Clarance up front. Daphne comes in a few minutes after Mark. She checks in with Clarance and then comes back to start working on the beverages. Maybe she also had a positive encounter with Clarance, because the three of us chat companionably while we work. She's wearing a black A-line dress with a dark green border around the hem and neckline and a cute little green bow in her hair; it's a great look on her.

Jeremy and I start transporting dishes to the Main Gallery and set them on the black-clothed table in the corner that Mark directs us to. Then Daphne and I lug the ice bucket and other beverage accoutrements out and place everything appealingly. After that's done, I take a moment to look around at the gallery.

I have to admit, I'm impressed. Clarance has a good eye for creating atmosphere. He has moved some of the displays to increase mingling areas and has strung white fairy lights from the ceiling. There are tiny tealight candles placed in strategically unbumpable areas around the room for added mood lighting. He has switched off the fluorescent overhead lights. With only the wall sconces on, the whole lighting effect creates a softer ambiance than normal.

Cottontail, where Bryce's art is located, has the strip lighting placed perfectly to illuminate his pieces, and an extra floor lamp has been added to increase the overall illumination without making the room jarringly brighter than the Main Gallery. There are several sound speakers throughout, and Clarance has them set to play classical jazz. Altogether, it's festive and classy.

Mark is also looking around admiringly. He turns to Clarance, who is fiddling with a candle that's sputtering. "It looks great, Clarance!"

Daphne and I chime in with agreement.

Clarance flushes and looks embarrassed but manages to get a weak "thank you" out. Jeremy catches my eye and winks, making my heart flutter.

I look at my watch and see it's almost time to open the doors.

The reception is perfect. It's well attended, and Bryce is resplendent in a blue silk shirt and black jeans. He's basking in the attention and enjoying telling guests about his work. I've been managing the desk up front, and already four of his prints have sold and one of his smaller canvas paintings. I'm glad our ideas are bearing fruit; Bryce will be pleased when he finds out. The art world is such an experiment of trial and error, it's gratifying when ideas pan out.

Daphne comes over during a lull in sales and sits on the edge of the desk. "Tonight's been good," she says, smiling happily. It's a relief to see her cheerful again.

"Yes, it has. Bryce seems ecstatic."

"He does, but I didn't mean that. A little bit ago, Clarance told me that he made the new schedule plans without considering obligations we might have. He apologized for the worry he caused me. Next week, he wants all four of us to sit down together and discuss new hours for The Palette to be open and how we can manage staffing." I gape at her, and she laughs. "Clarance does seem to be working to make amends, Val."

I look at her askance. "He does, and it's throwing me off. I'd gotten used to disliking him. I don't know what to make of this reasonable person who replaced him." We laugh together, happy our fourth coworker isn't quite such a terrible addition anymore.

Surprisingly, Mrs. Leonard is in attendance. I didn't think we would see her again after the mess Clarance made of her display. She comes up to me while I'm standing in a secluded corner sipping a drink.

"Valancy, isn't it?" she asks.

"Yes, ma'am. Are you enjoying the event, Mrs. Leonard?"

She scoffs. "You and Mark are both the same, insisting on calling me 'Mrs. Leonard.'" She looks mildly annoyed but doesn't ask me to call her something else. "Did that new person, Clarance"—she grimaces—"plan this event?"

Carefully, since I don't know where this is going, I nod. "Yes, he did."

"Well, he did a nice job. He certainly rubbed me the wrong way initially, but I can understand that people make mistakes. Maybe there's hope for him yet. He sent me such a nice apology and said since he was new, he hadn't realized how vital I am to the art scene. It was a little grandiose, but sometimes folks need to grovel a bit." She smiles at me. "I'm glad things got rectified. I'll bring my items back next week, if that works?"

"That's wonderful!" I'm relieved. "We'll get you all situated nicely. Thank you for your patience."

"Of course, my dear." She pats my arm and finds another guest to talk to.

The reception has thinned out, but we still have about half an hour remaining. Bryce is sitting on a chair outside Cottontail, and Ms. Galaxy is perched on a chair next to him, gushing about his art, holding a small piece she bought. They've been chatting with each other all evening and seem to be hitting it off. I think they're both lonely, and I'm happy to see they're making friends with each other. Maybe things will blossom between them.

Jeremy is talking to a pair from out of town who stopped by for the opening.

I walk over to where Clarance is holding up the wall, his

arms crossed comfortably. He looks tired but pleased. He smiles as I walk up. "Do you think it's been a successful event?" he asks. I'm sure he already knows it but wants confirmation.

"I do. You did a beautiful job coordinating everything, and we've had lots of sales. It's a success. You did a great job." I smile frankly at him.

He looks uncomfortable with the praise but accepts it.

"Also, Daphne told me about the changes to schedules, and Mrs. Leonard mentioned your heartfelt apology. Thank you for fixing those too, I know it matters to them."

He looks down at his shoes. When he looks back up, his expression is firm. "Valancy, I want to say thank you for telling me off."

My face heats up and my jaw drops.

He continues. "I think I needed someone to tell me I'd screwed up and why that mattered. I've been sent to other locations to make improvements, and I always do whatever I think is best. I never connect with the employees there, and while they never have seemed particularly pleased with my ideas, they've always gone along with them. Until you reproached at me, I'd never considered that the decisions I was making might be harmful. I was consumed with metrics and performance, and I'd lost sight that art galleries are about the people, the art, and the community. You reminded me, and it's a lesson I will remember whether I stay here or transfer somewhere else."

"That makes sense. I'm sorry, though, that I lost my temper with you. I feel bad about that. I could've tried harder to connect with you more professionally without yelling."

"Thinking over our prior interactions, I realized you had made many overtures of kindness to me, and I rejected all of them. I don't think I presented myself as someone who was welcoming of ideas."

He's not wrong. "I think we can agree, then, that mistakes were made by all involved, but that things are going better now. The future seems promising." I hold out my hand.

He takes it and we shake, a much more promising handshake this time. We smile at each other.

"Agreed."

It's late when Jeremy and I finally leave. The five of us cleaned up after the reception and then we all made plates of leftovers and sat on the patio, nibbling and laughing together. Daphne was the first to realize the time and said she had to leave in order to kiss Fred goodnight. The rest of us follow soon after her.

We sigh contentedly as we settle into our seats in Jeremy's car. My feet are aching in spite of my low heels and it's good to finally relax.

Jeremy looks over at me. "Do you still want to get food or ice cream?"

I can't say I'm hungry, but this evening feels like one of those rare, perfect moments where it feels like a waste not to extend it as long as possible because it's times like these when nothing can go wrong. "Sure! Let's go to Cosmina's and get ice cream. They have pretty outdoor seating."

Cosmina's Ice Cream Parlor isn't busy this late at night. It's only us on their raised wooden patio. The yellow umbrellas are still up, and strings of light bulbs illuminate the deck with a warm glow. We sit side by side at a high-top table in the corner.

Jeremy licks a spoonful of mint chip ice cream and closes his eyes in enjoyment. "Mm, this is perfect."

I take a bite of my banana cream pie ice cream and agree wholeheartedly. We sit and enjoy our treats, letting conversation pause.

"Jeremy?"

"Mhmm?" He looks over at me, his spoon in his mouth.

"I-I just wanted you to know that I think I could move forward with things." My pulse is racing. "If you want to," I add hastily.

His eyes gaze into mine, then drop to my lips, then rake back up to my eyes. "I would love that." He pauses. "Are you sure you're ready? Are things getting better with your dreams?"

"I think so. I can feel them having less of a pull on me, and other dreams are filtering in more often now. I think it's just a matter of time before Adrian is gone forever."

"You're sad about that." It's not a question.

I sigh, looking out into the darkness surrounding us. "It's hard not to be. But I'm also glad to be able to focus more firmly on the real world around me." I turn back to him. "On us." I take his hand. "This. This is what I've wanted for as long as I can remember. I'll never choose an imaginary reality over what's sitting right in front of me."

His eyes are soft as he looks at me. He raises his other hand to the side of my face and brushes stray hairs back from my cheek. "I'm glad we finally lined up with each other," he says softly.

"Me too." I lean over as much as my tall stool will allow, and he meets my lips halfway. The feel of his kiss takes my breath away. He tastes like mint. It feels like I've waited all my life for this moment, but also for all the beautiful moments yet to come.

All light disappears. I'm unsure how long the darkness lasts but suddenly, I'm stepping off the escalator onto the familiar greensward. I breathe a sigh of relief, taking a moment to look around at the view I love: The mismatched skyline of rainbow buildings. The Ferris wheel paused to let on more passengers. The swings. It has been such a joy to come here and be washed in perpetual sunsets. Or almost-always sunsets.

This time, it's twilight. The sun has set behind the hills. The sky is still dimly lit, but stars are starting to emerge. It reminds me of the magical night on top of the skyscraper. I've always thought the never-ending sunsets were beautiful, but the evening is wonderful too. It's quieter without as many people wandering around, and the colors are muted and velvety.

"You're here."

I whirl and the skirt of my dress fans out. Smiling, I reach out to Adrian. He grins back and grasps my hands tightly. For a moment, we let whatever this might have been between us just be; time to pause and savor that potential before it's gone forever, pleased that we're here and gifted another moment together.

The moment passes, and our smiles shift slightly and monumentally into something else. We know what's coming.

"I've been waiting for you," he says, no longer able to meet my eyes.

"I know. I'm glad I was able to come once more."

He glances up. "I was afraid you'd never come again."

"I think this is the last time. I can feel it. Whatever this was"—I stretch my arm out encompassing all the scape—"it's over for me. For us." I put my hand tenderly on his chest, leaning into him.

He looks into my eyes and nods.

"Something's changed… elsewhere… I can feel it." I say uncertainly. "I think that'll inhibit me from coming here again. I wanted to tell you that I don't want you to look for me or wait for me to appear."

He looks away, toward the Ferris wheel rising above the skyline.

I reach out and turn his face back to me, holding my hand

against his cheek. "Promise me, Adrian, that you'll go to a new scape that has nothing to do with me, and that you'll never try to find me again. I want to know you'll move on and live your life well. We were given a gift, but now we need to move on and not pine for what cannot be."

He exhales with effort and inclines his head in acknowledgement, resting his forehead against mine. If his eyes are anything like mine, they have tears in them. "I promise I'll try to move on, but I'm going to miss you," he says chokingly. "You've changed my life."

Now it's my turn to take a shuddering breath. "You've changed my life too." I reach my arms up and wrap them around his neck. I feel his arms around my waist, his fingers digging into my sides. I sob and I feel his shoulders shake.

I turn my head to press a kiss to his cheek and whisper in his ear, "Goodbye, Adrian."

"Goodbye, my Valancy."

Chapter 24

ADRIAN

She's gone. I can still feel the touch of her kiss on my cheek, the dampness of her tears and mine on my skin. Her warmth. Immediately, I think of how I can find her again, but I stop myself. No, she's right: there was never going to be a happy ending for us. There is only an ending, but we got to say goodbye, and that is something to cherish.

I turn in the direction of the housing district and plod slowly home. The scape is aloofly returning to baseline. I pause for a moment to watch the city, the rides, and the candy vista as they revert. Watching what's left of Valancy leave breaks my heart all over again, but I can't look away. I'll never see these places quite like this again. She made my world the most beautiful it has ever been, and I want to see every last bit of it that I can before it's gone forever.

Minutes pass and at last, the transition is over. The city has closed up shop for the night, and everything is soaked in austere darkness. The sun will rise again tomorrow, but I can't imagine it will shine as brightly. I wipe my eyes and turn toward home again.

My bedroom is bathed in soft morning light. I lie there stunned for a moment, before reaching up to my damp cheeks and wiping my eyes. It's over. He's gone. I feel it deep within myself that I'll never see Adrian in my dreams again. For once, I try not to overthink and allow myself to grieve. More tears threaten to puddle in my ears.

A thud at the foot of the bed alerts me to Bob's arrival, and I roll onto my side to pet him. I turn my head into the pillow to dry my eyes. I take a deep breath and savor this moment, where I can still remember my dream before the reality of my life comes back full force. I wipe my eyes again, thinking of Adrian.

What if I forget him entirely? I feel a wave of panic at the thought, since it's not unrealistic to think that might happen; dreams do fade quickly. How can I preserve his memory?

An idea comes to me, and with it, a feeling of purpose. It's not too late.

I get out of bed, dabbing the last moisture from my face and out of my ears with the sleeve of my pajama top. I take my laptop off the desk and bring it back to my bed. I flip through my dream journal and quickly add my final entry. I look through it, reliving the memories. I start to type.

ADRIAN

The walk does me good. The air is fresh and cool and soothing to the ache in my heart. I open the door to my apartment and lean heavily against it after it closes. What do I do now? *Grieve.* The word comes to me, and it feels fitting. I'm allowed to not be okay.

I turn on the light and head for the kitchen. Something on the wall catches my eye and I stop.

The sign. It's finally here.

I walk over to it and run my fingers along the wood finish. It's perfect. It matches the décor of my apartment exquisitely, and the blue letters complement the brown wood. But the letters don't say "*Welcome Home*" as Valancy had specified. Instead, in looping font, they read "*Savor Each Moment.*" I run my finger over the words. Yes, Valancy, you taught me to appreciate this existence. To look forward to what comes next with anticipation. Maybe there *is* more to be excited about even though my time with you is over.

I go to the window and look out at the scape. Its dark silhouettes feel more full of potential than they did a minute ago. Valancy told me not to stay here and wait for her. But what if I stay because I want to? This scape has become important to me, and I've connected with it like I never have with a scape before.

I don't think she meant I couldn't stay, but that I shouldn't if it would make it harder for me to live my life well. But maybe here is where I need to be to continue to live my life fully.

Starting to get my thoughts down on paper has helped bring closure. Also, in the perpetually annoying way of dreams, they fade from memory quickly. Although I can recall the feeling of sadness, it's insulated by the overwhelming amount of real-world sensations. It's not callousness that allows me to turn my thoughts to Jeremy and our kiss, but simply the nature of dreams and memory.

I smile fondly as I think of kissing Jeremy last night at Cosmina's and again on our front doorstep when we got home. We parted inside the front door, taking things slow as we're still unsure of what our new future together means.

Jeremy has been running errands with his mom all day. He has sent me some sweet texts, but otherwise I've just been waiting for him to get home.

The need for writing out my thoughts has passed. I turn to my Ferris wheel artwork, which is almost done.

Jeremy peeks into my room when he comes home. I drop my brush and run over to him, wrapping my arms around him.

"I'm glad you're home. I missed you."

His arms wrap around me in return, and his reply is muffled

in my hair. "Me too."

After a minute, I pull away to look up at him. "I want to finish my piece and do a quick yoga session, but then do you want to make dinner and watch an episode?"

"I think it's the season finale. Do you want to watch two so we can skip the likely cliffhanger?"

"That sounds good to me. Avoiding suspense, even from fictional sources, sounds like a friendly choice for my mental health."

As I touch some final glimmering dots of paint to the canvas to convey light, my mind drifts back to Adrian. I try not to think about whether it's rational or not, but I hope he'll be okay.

Chapter 25

VALANCY

Work has improved. There is still an underlying reticence around Clarance. After all, it's hard to move forward when someone has behaved poorly and uncomfortable conversations were had, but hope is there where it wasn't before. I miss our old dynamic, and I probably always will, but I can see Clarance fitting in with us and maybe even becoming our friend if he stays long enough. I'm shocked to find myself thinking that too.

Apparently, Clarance has some digestive issues that react poorly to certain foods. That's why he was rude about those blueberry muffins I brought in. Of course, that's no excuse for being impolite, but I let bygones be bygones and ask him the types of items he enjoys eating. Depending on what the bakery has in stock, I should be able to regularly include him. He also assured me that he won't be upset if I can't always accommodate his restrictions; he'll still join us on the patio with his tomato juice. I'm trying hard not to judge his beverage of choice.

His sitter brought his daughter by on Tuesday after school, and she ran around admiring everything. Jillian's a cute kid and apparently has a penchant for kitties. Her dress is pink with red hearts and disembodied cat heads.

The juxtaposition between her lithe enthusiasm and her awkward dad makes me smile. Jillian takes after him in some features, like his serious gray eyes, but not the ones that make him seem uncomfortable in his body. She's slender with thick, brown hair in a long braid down her back. If I have my guess, I don't think she'll grow up to be unduly tall and lanky either. More power to the other half of her genetics.

Clarance told me she has wanted to see where he works for a long time, but he has never brought her to any of the galleries he has been assigned to before. I think that's a promising sign for how he feels about The Palette in comparison.

Clarance and I are standing near the front desk, watching Mark give Jillian a very formal grown-up tour of the Main Gallery. She's loving the attention and gives him serious adult responses when he asks her questions.

"She's adorable." I say, turning to Clarance.

"Thanks." He smiles at me. "She's had a tough time, moving so much, but she seems to be adjusting here. Her nightmares have stopped."

"Nightmares?" I'm always curious to hear about other people's dream experiences.

"Yeah, she rode a Ferris wheel at a carnival a few years ago. I thought a Ferris wheel would be a good choice for a little kid, but I guess the height scared her. For a few years, she had these recurring nightmares of riding enormous Ferris wheels. She'd wake up screaming. It was awful."

"I'm sorry," I say sympathetically. "That must have been hard."

"It was. But recently they stopped. She hasn't had one in a couple weeks, and she even expressed interest in going to the fair when it's in town. Maybe she's gotten past it."

"That's great! I hope so."

Epilogue

VALANCY

It has been two weeks since my last dream of Adrian. It has been unsettling that my memories of him faded quickly despite, or maybe because of, my efforts to hold onto them. I mentally curse that he lived in my mind and is bound by the laws that govern dreams, not those of the real world.

I'm grateful that Jeremy suggested a sleep journal early on, because I was able to capture the narrative of our interactions in a permanent way. Reading back over my entries feels surreal, as though I'm reading about someone else's experiences. The details I read are gone from my memory, but I know I didn't make them up.

Jeremy walks into my room without knocking and hands me a hot tea. He has been particularly sweet and gentle with me lately. He knows that I've been having a difficult time accepting what happened to me.

"Here," he says. "I think I made it the way you like it."

I take a sip. It could be a smidge sweeter, but it's quite drinkable. "It's good, thank you, love."

"How're you doing?"

I smile. "Better, actually. You remember how I teased you about turning my dreams into a novel? Well, I think I might. Not a lurid one, but a regular one. I barely remember some of these things, but if I find it interesting to read about, maybe other people would too. I've been working on an outline."

His face relaxes. I think he has been worried about me. "That sounds great! You've mentioned for years that you wanted to write a novel, along with all your other creative goals." He sounds proud of me. "This is the perfect way to achieve that and honor this time in your life."

I'm grateful he understands and has been able to accept this side of me. "Thank you, that's exactly how I feel about it too."

He leans over and gives me a kiss. I still adore every touch we share. I waited so long for this.

***

Valancy hasn't returned, and many guests have come and gone since the last time we saw each other. I'm finally convinced she's gone for good. Part of me does want to keep waiting for her forever, but a much bigger part of me agrees that I need to move on. I've tried to take some time to process and heal in order to proceed with my life in a healthy way.

When no visitors are in the scape, I've taken to using the downtime to walk around. It's not the same as when Valancy worked her magic here, but it's better than seeing it under the guise of someone else's perception. In its neutral state, I can more easily drape it in my memories.

I pass the bar where we ate and see a light on. That's unusual. I push on the door and it opens. Frieda hurries out with a menu, looking frazzled, but relaxes when she sees it's only me.

"Oh hi, Adrian. I thought maybe it was a customer and I'd missed a notification."

"Hey, Frieda. Sorry to rattle you. I saw the light."

"Of course, come in." She motions me to the room she came from. I follow her into a space in the back that reminds me of my apartment both in color and lack of décor.

"You live here?" I'm surprised. "I thought everyone lived in the housing complex."

"Yes. Since I'm assigned to a particular building in a scape, I get to live adjacent to it."

"Get to," I reply sarcastically.

She frowns at me. "Yes, I get to. I like it."

I feel remorseful for my sarcastic tone.

"Are you all right?" she asks.

"I will be." I sit down on a comfortable blue armchair, and she hands me a hot cup of coffee.

"Is it about that woman with the dark red hair?"

I nod.

"She hasn't been here lately, has she?"

I shake my head, sipping my drink.

"Ah, that must be hard."

"It is."

"Have you thought about asking for a transfer somewhere else?"

"I did at first, but I think I want to stay. This place is special to me now because of her."

"I can understand that."

"Can you?"

"Dude, I run a bar and café. I haven't had your experience of a repeat customer that I connected with, but I've often heard stories from guests. I know how a person can become part of your feeling of home. So, you're going to stay?"

"I think so. It's hard now, but I'm going to try. I think it will be worth it."

"Why don't you ask to move into the scape?"

I immediately balk at the idea. Valancy's sign is still up at my apartment, and I'm sure I couldn't move that with me. "No, I wouldn't want to give up my place."

She looks like she's thinking about trying to argue her

point, but something in my face must change her mind. "If you're interested, sometimes when we're between shifts a few of us get together. You're welcome to join us."

"What do you do?"

"The scape is completely useable even though it's in neutral. Some of us decided it would be fun to enjoy it. Like riding the wheel, having picnics in the park, things like that. We'd love to add you to our group."

My heart lightens. For the first time since Valancy left, I have the prospect of real companionship and connection.

***

Life goes on.

I make a point of stopping by Frieda's place to hang out after guests have left. Sometimes it's only the two of us, but often there are others. Soon I'm regularly spending time with Mary from the shoe shop, Raul, Preeta, and Ti as well. I can't believe I've been here this long without ever trying to connect with anyone else. Having friends has made the evenings enjoyable, but it has also made work more enjoyable too.

Ti tends to work near the wheel, Raul has a food stand in the shopping district, and Preeta is the same as me and isn't assigned a specific area. Mary is assigned to the building where Valancy manifested the shoe store. I see them often during my work and even though we don't interact with each other, it's still nice to share a look of camaraderie when we pass.

***

It's late. The six of us were all in attendance tonight, and we went to the swings and then got enormous cotton candies. My face is sticky, and I feel happy as I head back to my housing district. I get to the arch that Valancy and I went through when she came to see my place. I pause and look around. It's the same as it always is, but it will forever be more because of her. I imagine her walking tentatively through, then whirling and laughing with joy. I run my hand over the bricks and smile. It's a good memory.

I continue on my way and unlock the door to my apartment. I'm thinking about a story Raul was telling us earlier and only give Valancy's sign a cursory glance, just to make sure it's still there, before heading to the kitchen. I'm not very hungry. The cotton candy spoiled my appetite, but a small snack that isn't sweet would be good. I eat my food and stare out at the scape, still bathed in darkness, waiting for our next visitor.

I look at the landmarks I know better than the back of my hand. The memories are now a blend of moments with Valancy and those with my new friends. I still hang onto her memory, afraid to let it go, but I'll admit that more and more the memories that come first to my mind are newer ones she's not part of. This bothered me at first, until I realized that I have these new memories because of her. In a way, they're Valancy memories too, since she taught me how to live my life.

I'll be tired tomorrow if I don't sleep soon. I prep for bed and slide between the sheets. The last thing I think of before drifting off is how eager I am for tomorrow.

I walk across the parking lot, approaching the front door. An elderly gentleman in a bright floral shirt is sitting on a bench out front. He greets me with a casual "howdy" and a toothy smile as I approach the building, then turns back to his newspaper.

As I walk in, a bell rings. A slender man sits behind the desk. He looks up and gives me a cursory smile and welcomes me.

I'm in an art gallery. Hundreds of artworks cover the walls, bombarding me with all manner of designs and colors. I browse around, picking up figurines and admiring handiwork. A middle-aged man is busy behind the jewelry counter, but he greets me pleasantly before continuing with his work. Another employee, a young woman, is helping someone else decide on an artwork; I think the green one is nicer.

From the main area are arched doorways leading to smaller galleries. I move into the first one that has a copper rabbit over the doorway and admire the floral paintings on display. The next one is full of ceramic mugs, shaped invitingly for a hot beverage.

As I enter the third gallery, I pause. Facing me is a large painting of a Ferris wheel illuminated above a dark cityscape. It's surreal and haunting. As I look around, I see more magical scenes. One is a girl spinning on a swing ride, her hair and dress billowing around her, a look of pure joy on her face. Another is of a goldfish in a pond swimming around two sets of toes. The next is a massive pile of onion rings. The opposite wall has a huge piece depicting a purple bull with steaming nostrils. A smashed tea set flies all around him. This last one makes me chuckle.

"Do you like them?" a quiet voice behind me asks.

I turn and see a woman standing in the doorway. She's pleasant-looking, with long, dark red hair tied back in a high ponytail. She's wearing baggy jeans and a loose blouse. I smile at her. "I think they're wonderful."

Her eyes hold mine, a slight question about her brows. She seems to shake herself and regains her composure. "Thank you, they're mine."

"What was the inspiration?"

She twists her hands together showing her discomfort. "My dreams," she says hesitantly.

I want to put her at ease, assure her I'm not judging her inspiration. "You must have wonderful dreams."

"Yes," she says wistfully, looking at a canvas of a pink milkshake with two straws. "They were wonderful." She turns back to me and smiles, still a look of doubt in her eyes that she tamps down. "Enjoy looking around, and let us know if you need any assistance." Her professional tone is back.

"Thank you, I will." My eyes follow her as she leaves, her ponytail swaying slightly.

I turn back to look at a painting of two people standing on a rooftop, surrounded by fairy lights and fireflies. What wonderful dreams she must have had. I move to the next one, but instead I see only the walls of my bedroom and sunlight from the scape streaming in my window.

I gasp. The details of the dream linger in my mind for a moment. There was something—no, someone. I try to hang onto it, but I can't. It's gone. I'm left with a feeling of emptiness, as though I've forgotten something important.

After a minute, the feeling fades and I get up. Sometimes I think it would be nice if I could remember my dreams, but maybe it's just as well I must face my life as it is.

"Did he leave?"

"Did who leave?" asks Clarance, who's sitting at the front desk today.

"That man, the one with the bomber jacket."

Clarance shrugs. "I don't know, it's been busy."

I feel frustrated, but I'm not sure why. I came upon a young man in Roadrunner where my pieces are on display. He seemed familiar, but I couldn't place him. Déjà vu, maybe. Maybe he'll come in again. I put it from my mind and turn back to Clarance.

"You wanted to plan my reception, right?"

He hesitates. Sometimes he still worries about stepping on our toes. "If you want me to."

"Absolutely! You did a fantastic job with the Torres Sisters and Mr. Ezekiel, and I want only the best for my show." I wink at him.

He smiles, clearly delighted at the praise. "Wonderful! I've been thinking of some ideas."

I walk back into my gallery and look around. Adrian's and my memories, if they can even be called that, fill the walls. Jeremy's comment about painting other moments of my dreams inspired me to create more visual interpretations of my experience in the scape. Of course, they could never do it justice, but the effort helped bring me closure, along with beginning to draft my book, which I'm still working on.

When I finished enough pieces for a show, I pitched the idea to Clarance and Mark, and they enthusiastically agreed. The public response to my artworks has been extremely positive, and the local paper told me they're planning to attend my reception next week. We'll see what happens from there.

My phone vibrates, and I pull it out of my pocket. It's from Jeremy asking if I want to meet him for dinner after work at a new restaurant downtown. I smile and let him to know what time I'll be there.

I'm happy.

Being with Jeremy is all I'd ever hoped it would be. And to be honest, I think we're better now than we ever would've been in the past. Part of me thinks about the time we missed, but I remember that we didn't really miss anything because we've always been part of each other's lives. We had to grow independently and together and both be ready for this step at the same time. It was worth the wait. Maybe my next series of paintings will be about our love story.

The End

About the Author

M. Rose Elliott is an author and professional artist who works in a museum and volunteers at her local art collective. She loves to read, make art, dance, watch sci-fi, and explore the world around her. She lives in New Mexico with her husband and cats. *Dreaming Outside the Lines* is her debut novel. Connect with her via email at Author.M.Rose.Elliott@gmail.com or on Instagram @Author.M.Rose.Elliott.

Acknowledgements

Fourteen years ago, I told myself I was going to write a novel. Ever since then, I've been waiting to think of a plot. Finally, two years ago I had a vivid dream, and when I woke up, I knew it would be the inspiration for this book.

Of course, this story has grown and become much more than I initially imagined, in part because of the wonderful assistance and support I've had throughout the writing process.

I'm grateful to Dylan, Laura, and Shannon for reading my very rough first draft and giving me their feedback and thoughts so generously. Your support encouraged me to continue on.

Sandi's feedback on my second draft had profound impacts on the plot. Jeremy's character exists because of you. I'm glad we connected and became part of each other's writing journeys.

Shannon and Sandi also willingly read my third draft, for which I am so appreciative. I know it's hard to reread a story, but getting the progressive feedback was extremely helpful.

Thank you, Robert, for finding out I was writing a novel, proactively asking to read it, and then providing me such helpful feedback and answering all of my many questions. This story improved because of your insight, despite this not being your normal preferred genre.

Richard, thank you for giving my book one last read-through before it headed to publishing. It was the best feeling when you told me you loved it.

I would be remiss if I did not mention the Valencia County Writers Group. I was feeling very disheartened by the writing process when I first saw your group mentioned in the newspaper. I decided to give it a try, and I'm glad I did. Critiquing five pages at a time doesn't sound like a lot, but it was enough to get me writing and revising. Additionally, your unwavering and enthusiastic support for my project helped motivate me to finish it. I'm honored you shared your writing and personal projects with me, and I hope you all know how much I appreciate your help with mine.

Of course, I need to mention the professionals who assisted me in my publication process. Donna Marie West for her thoughtful and thorough editing and advice. Sabrina Watts of Enchanted Ink Studio | www.enchantedinkstudio.com for creating a cover that is exactly what I wanted for my book. Aubrey Labitigan of Jai Design | www.facebook.com/designjai ensured that the inside of my book was as beautiful as the outside with interior formatting and graphic designs. All of you were kind to me as I navigated the new world of self-publishing and made sure I was happy with the final result. Thank you.

To my mom—who only just found out about this project—I want to thank you for your unwavering support of my creative projects. You always seem a bit surprised when I tell you what I'm accomplishing creatively, but I know you're always proud of me. That means so much to me.

And finally, thank you to my husband, Christopher. I appreciate your support of this project, your advice, thoughts, and suggestions. Being able to run ideas by you and vent about how tedious the writing process is has helped me get here.

Less thanks to Teak and Dot since you girls mostly served to distract me from writing, in the cutest ways possible. Bob is inspired by you.

Thank you to all who read this book, it means the world to me that I get to share this story with you. I would appreciate your honest review, if you have time to leave one.

www.ingramcontent.com/pod-product-compliance
Lightning Source LLC
LaVergne TN
LVHW041906070526
838199LV00051BA/2512